TRUE NORTH

TRUE NORTH

Heather Ehrman Krill

authorHOUSE®

AuthorHouse™
1663 Liberty Drive
Bloomington, IN 47403
www.authorhouse.com
Phone: 1 (800) 839-8640

Published by AuthorHouse 11/06/2015

ISBN: 978-1-5049-5904-9 (sc)
ISBN: 978-1-5049-5905-6 (hc)
ISBN: 978-1-5049-5903-2 (e)

Library of Congress Control Number: 2015918008

To my village,
especially Carver and Greta,
whose stories have yet to unfold

FOREWORD

Since 1978, when the first baby was born through in vitro fertilization, there have been about five million births achieved this way around the world. My husband, Geoff, and I conceived both of our children, now five and four, with the help of the Dartmouth-Hitchcock Fertility Clinic. We were not sure children would ever happen for us, due to a spinal cord injury he sustained twenty years ago. However, we were extremely lucky, and were gifted Carver Gregory and Greta Paige.

Afterward, we faced the decision of what to do with our ten remaining frozen embryos, which by definition are fertilized eggs. We made the choice to make them available for other families like ours. We don't know if births resulted from any of those embryos, nor do we know anything about the family that took them on as their own, hoping for life as we had done so desperately years before.

But we wondered about them, and so I wrote this novel about the potential for life. It's all any of us has, after all.

ACKNOWLEDGMENTS

First, I would like to thank Rotary International District 7850 for granting me a scholarship to write this novel through an independent study at Plymouth State University. The local Lincoln Woodstock Rotary, its members and ideals, were instrumental in my pursuit of this professional goal. Thank you to Meg Peterson, director of the National Writing Project in New Hampshire and professor of English at PSU, who worked as my literary adviser and sounding board.

Thank you to Robert Nelson, my principal at Lin-Wood Public School in Lincoln, New Hampshire, who supported my crazy notion that I could be a full-time English teacher and write a novel in one year. Thanks also to Kelly Nelson, my teaching friend, and three of my then-sophomore students, Pearce Bourassa, Eunice Bartlett, and Ryan Clermont, for each writing a letter of recommendation so that I could even apply for the Rotary Teacher Scholarship.

Thank you to Kathy Seidel-Slango, my first-grade teacher, for teaching me the magic of reading books and for editing early drafts of *True North* for me; to Tom Gotsill, my American Lit teacher, for modeling for me what it means to be a teacher-writer and writer-teacher; and to all teachers for inspiring their students to work to their potential regardless of their age or ability.

Thank you to Lisa Callamaro for being the first professional in the field of publishing to tell me my idea was a good one. Thank you to the group of women in my friendship circle for reading early and later drafts, and for providing feedback, laughter, and childcare.

Thank you to Jennifer Whitcher for sharing your mad editorial skills; to the Lin-Wood Girls of Summer and Rebecca Steeves for writing with me in the White Mountains; to my AP classmates—Kayla Fadden, Eunice Bartlett, Colby Chase, Maria Spanos, Colbie Blaisdell, and Bailey Clermont—for being my most critical readers; to my other classes of students at Lin-Wood Public School for reading, commenting, and providing constructive criticism; and to my book club for endless encouragement and read-alouds.

Thank you to my village, the ones in my adolescence who pushed me or challenged me in ways that will forever impact the stories I write and the woman I have grown into, and to the local community of friends and family who contributed to my GoFundMe fundraiser so that I could pursue self-publishing through AuthorHouse. There are 104 people on that list, and I wish I could put them all here. You know who you are, and I'll be forever grateful for your donations. Thank you to AuthorHouse for giving me the kick in the pants to move forward with *True North.*

Thank you to the Lin-Wood Community Childcare Center for nurturing our children so I could be a writer. Thank you to Mom, Dad, Phil, Joyce, Greg, Holly, Allison, and Brian for being present physically and/or emotionally whenever we needed you to be. Thank you to my husband, Geoff, for believing I could write a book in less than a year and helping me to make it happen, and to our children, Carver and Greta, for loving good stories and having the best imaginations in the world.

PROLOGUE

Potential energy, as defined by Merriam Webster, is "the amount of energy a thing has because of its position or because of the arrangement of its parts."

One Young Man with a Very Old Soul

I was thirteen when I ended my life. It doesn't matter why at this point, except maybe to those I left behind all those years ago, including my sisters, brothers, parents, and countless relatives and friends. Why did I take my own life? I could say I was being bullied, or struggling with my sexual identity, or couldn't handle living with my mentally ill mother or dealing with a depression so deep that living was not a viable option. I could say that I'm happier here in heaven, because I no longer feel sad, but that would not be the complete truth. I simply don't feel anything here, and I'm ready to give the living world another try. I fully understand why we might not have a choice in the family we end up with, but if I could make one request, I would like to have a brother or a sister. I think that's important.

One Young Woman with a Very Old Soul

I was twelve when leukemia ended my life. At the time, it was surprising that I would die in that moment, when I had battled death many times and always pulled through. Mostly, I miss my parents and my friends from school. Kids don't realize how good they have it until it's too late and they become adults. Or they don't become anything because something happens that takes them away before they reach their potential, what they could become.

I think I would have made a good teacher, or maybe even a nurse, since I was lucky enough to have so many on my team, helping me to fight my fight against the cancer that ultimately took my last breath. Looking back from up here, if I had the chance to live again, I would be a scientist or research biologist or even a doctor to help rid the world of all forms of cancer. I would be cool with being someone's only child again, but if I am destined to have more than one sibling, please let me be born first. That way I'll be someone's "only," even if just for a little while. I think that's important.

Another Young Man with a Very Old Soul

I was sixteen when a cardiac birth defect ended my life. Up to that moment, I had been living the dream: I was president of my class, the girls loved me, my friends loved me, and my family loved me. Don't get me wrong; life wasn't perfect. But I didn't have a lot to complain about, and I was headed in the right direction. My plan was to run for public office one day and make some big changes in our world, and people would have voted for me too. I had charisma, they told me, and lots of it.

And then, one morning, I didn't wake up. It was like a dream, watching from up above. Why couldn't I make my body move? Why couldn't I take a breath? Why would my mom have to find me like that in the morning? It didn't seem fair that something I didn't even know about could end my life before I was good and ready—or good and old.

In my next life, I'd like to reach some potential other than tenth grade and a driver's license. Also, I had a brother in my first life, and he was awesome, my best friend, really. But if living is all about new experiences, I would like to know what it's like to have a sister, even if she turns out to be a pain in the ass. I think that's important.

Another Young Woman with a Very Old Soul

I was fourteen when a teenage drunk driver ended my life. My friends and I were walking back from King Kone, which is on a busy main road in Merrimack. It was Friday night about nine, and we were walking to Olivia's house—a seemingly harmless activity for four freshmen in high school. I suppose we should have been on the other side of the road, but with Olivia's house so close, we stayed put. So we were walking with the traffic instead of against it.

So none of us saw the car drift over the white line and onto the grass. We were walking and laughing about an incident earlier in the day; I couldn't tell you what had been so funny. Olivia must have looked back, because I remember her screaming. Then I remember looking down on the scene of ambulances, plus dads who had been having ice cream with their kids and were trying to direct traffic.

It was too late for me, but they were able to save Olivia, Ella, and Hazel, who went on to reach their potential in life. They became a photographer, a social worker, and a marine biologists—and mothers. So I would really like to head back to the world and finish something important and be someone important to someone again. I would take on the role of daughter, son, brother, or sister—whatever you need me to be. But I would like to go back to New Hampshire if possible, as I really loved growing up there as a kid. That's my one request, if we are allowed to make requests. This isn't prison; it's heaven, so we should be able to make requests. I think that's important.

Inner Compass Instruction Manual
(Provided to each soul before returning to life on earth)

Materials needed:

One human body

One internal compass

Previous souls

An endless human support network

No assembly required

Directions for use:

1. Be ready to return for another life based on lives lived previously and lessons learned.

2. Have a sense of your "true north," which makes you ready to focus your attention on building relationships, taking on challenges, and pursuing your passion.

3. You are born with an internal compass within your soul. This compass stays with you throughout each lifetime. Its needle is in the direction you are to travel. There are times when you get off course or lose sight of true north. You may require support from the souls surrounding you in that time and place. You may also be supported by souls who lived in and around you in a previous lifetime. This occurs when the soul is energized by the lives lived in a different body, a different place, and with different people. However, sometimes a soul may continue to travel among

the same souls during different lifetimes. This is one facet of reincarnation.

4. At times, it may feel like a stranger is visiting in dreams, but this is the sensation of having an emotional echo or the vibration of having lived another life. You may feel as if someone is talking to you, advising you, and helping you to see the world in a different way. Remember, this is the body and soul's way of growing stronger with each life lived.

5. You won't remember having lived this past life and spending time in heaven. However, you will remember certain moments. This often happens through muscle memory: you feel you have ridden a bike before, assisted an elderly woman across the street, tasted joy on Christmas morning, or been betrayed by a good friend.

6. People depend on their faith and family, but you must also develop a trust in the internal compass that lives somewhere between you heart and your head. This inner strength is what sustains a soul on each trip back to earth and in the interim.

7. Some mountain roads pass through the height of the land. Years ago, only horses and the burliest of people traveled these pinnacles in the spirit of exploration. On a map, tiny lines with little space between them represent the steepest parts of the trail, where travel would be most difficult. As the spaces spread out, the trail becomes less steep, and the traveler is better able to enjoy the journey. Places exist like this all over in nature, where civilizations have built passages to peaks to catch glimpses from the very top of the world. There man and woman realize the ebb and flow of humanity—the mountains and valleys, the challenge

and opportunity, the loves and losses of life. But, in the chaos of living, we sometimes forget and need gentle reminders to sojourn on toward our true north.

8. Teenagers, especially, can be tricky. Surviving adolescence is just a matter of degrees. It's one thing to get off course for a little while and then be pulled back by your true north—that ever-important internal compass. However, if a teen continues off course for a mile or more, finding his or her way back is far more difficult because the distance between true north and magnetic north- the direction of travel- grows greater. Yet if teenagers are resourceful and don't give up, signs and people can help them to reorient themselves to the right course, the forward direction of travel, the path they are meant to travel.

9. Losing your way in the world is scary. If possible, view the world from the top of a mountain on a clear, starry night or bright morning, and remember that you have lived before and will live again.

10. Finally, find true north and continue in that direction. Stop and rest, and follow rivers for a while, but always trust that you will find the path again. Also allow the souls nearby to support this process. Onward!

1

Kinetic energy is the energy associated with motion.

Andrew

When I was first paralyzed back in high school, my initial thoughts were not, *Oh, shit, my legs don't move. Will I survive this? What will I do now that my legs don't work?* Instead, I wondered, *Will a girl ever want to date me? Will I be able to become a dad one day?*

Now I think back to that April day when my wife, Elizabeth, and I, having been blessed with our two children, decided to put our remaining embryos up for adoption. I felt that life couldn't get any better. I had been paralyzed in the prime of my young life, yet I had proven resilient. I had established a career, lived a full life, married a smart, lovely woman, and even been able to father children. Life had been very good to me.

Jolene, our in vitro fertilization nurse and lifeline throughout the three-year fertility process, had explained that our remaining ten embryos could be given to an infertile couple, giving them the opportunity to have children. The alternative, called "discarding the embryos"—that is, throwing them away—didn't feel right. We had spent so many years trying to get pregnant without success due to my spinal cord injury, it seemed our best option was to pay it forward to help another family. When Dr. Carver, the psychologist assigned to assess our mental states, asked us to rate our attachment to the embryos, both Elizabeth and I settled on a two on a scale of one to ten—ten being not able to imagine the separation.

However, these embryos were not babies; they were simply the potential for life. Think about all the eggs released in the world each month that don't meet up with a sperm; or the egg who does meet a sperm creating an embryo, which for whatever reason, doesn't implant on the uterine lining; or actually implants but something isn't quite right and the embryo stops growing. Crazy, right, that I'm a man who thinks about egg release and embryo development, but I spent more time thinking about trying to have a baby than most men would admit to. If the conditions are right, and the egg fertilizes, there is the potential for life. But there is only a potential, because things sometimes happen that don't allow the embryo to become a healthy baby.

We were lucky. After three years of trying and thousands of dollars, our life potentials became babies, and our family was complete. Why wouldn't we want to help give another couple the chance to be parents?

Initially, Elizabeth worried that if we donated the embryos, one of our children might meet a genetically related siblings in college—or somewhere—and fall in love. That was a worst-case scenario, I told her.

Dr. Lincoln, our fertility specialist, explained that the adoption process would be anonymous; when we signed the paperwork agreeing to permit another couple to adopt our frozen embryos, we released them from everything, including our ever wanting them back as children. However, she went on to say, that didn't mean in ten or twenty years, the laws governing fertility and adoption couldn't change, and we might have someone knocking on our door to find out if we are his or her biological parents. We checked the box allowing Dartmouth Hitchcock Medical Center to contact us through the court system if one or more of our embryos grew into a child who later developed a medical condition requiring a genetic match for a donation, such as of an organ or bone marrow.

The heavy wooden chairs in Dr. Carver's office had green cushions. It was the same office we had sat in years earlier, when another doctor had determined we were "sound" enough to handle the up-and-down emotions and raging hormones that came with fertility treatments. Elizabeth teased me about fibbing on our initial screening when the doctor asked if there had been a history of mental illness in either of our families. I had been excited about the process of starting our new family and didn't want to lose focus by explaining the serious medical history, depression, alcoholism, and mental health disorders that ran amok in my family tree. A first cousin had committed suicide as a teenager. An aunt had been diagnosed with schizophrenia. Another first cousin had passed away in his sleep at only eighteen, and another from leukemia at twelve. I hadn't listed any of those on the form, a decision Elizabeth felt would come back to bite us.

However, in this most recent visit, the last question Dr. Carver asked us was whether we had any restrictions on the embryos. Did we care who adopted our embryos—like religious preference, for example?

"Of course not. Anybody who is okay with our professions, medical histories, etc., is welcome to choose our embryos," Elizabeth nervously rattled off, twisting her hands in her lap. Then she looked at me with her green eyes burning through my soul as if to say, "Please don't tell her what you really think!"

I mulled it over for a moment and chose to keep quiet, thinking it would be unlikely that a gay couple would go through all that trouble. I'm not homophobic, although Elizabeth would argue otherwise. I just don't like to talk about homosexuality, as a matter of principle. I was excited to help another heterosexual man or woman who did not want to adopt a baby but really wanted his or her own biological child. Call it survival of the fittest or testosterone overload. Men and woman are supposed to have babies, but this doesn't mean I don't like gay people.

I'm a consultant for accessibility and help businesses meet standard building codes. That doesn't sound as exciting as being a professional athlete or rock star, but I do travel quite a bit and feel good about overcoming my disability. So, in my line of work, I meet people I think might be gay, but we don't have to talk about the lifestyle, and I'm cool with that.

However, Elizabeth thinks I don't believe gay or lesbian people should raise children. I haven't said that to her exactly, but my inability to express thoughts clearly on the matter over the years has left her to assume the worst. This isn't exactly the case, but I don't wish to discuss the issue with her—and it's not because I think I might be gay and am afraid to be found out. That would be ridiculous. It's more complicated than that, so I let her think she has me all figured out, since we've been married for more than twenty years. She's made me promise not to "indoctrinate" our children, as she calls it, with that kind of talk. It's one of the few areas in our marriage where we don't agree—along with the fact that she thinks I work too much.

Being in the consulting business, I work many late nights on the phone or my computer, and I travel frequently. There was a time she encouraged my business travel, encouraging my passion for what I do, especially before we had children. She worked a lot too and loved to be by herself. But once we had two little ones, much of the parenting duties fell on her, and I understood she was tired after working all day. I always did what I could, but chasing toddlers and keeping them safe isn't easy for someone in a wheelchair, something Elizabeth seemed to forget from time to time.

However, if a loving couple wanted to raise our embryos—those life potentials—I wished them every bit of luck. Raising kids isn't easy, and I've never been one to shy away from a challenge.

After I was hurt and needed a wheelchair to get around, I was convinced girls wouldn't want to date me and that I'd probably never get to be a dad. I was still recovering from my injury when everyone else went off to college or the military or started working. Once I regained my confidence, I took a few classes at the community college and started advising local businesses on how they could be more accessible for people with disabilities. Time passed quickly, my little business grew, and I found myself with no shortage of women to date. The wheelchair didn't bother them at all, and it was fun for a while.

People were funny about the chair at times, infuriating at others. For example, one girlfriend would pump gas into my car for me just because it was a pain for me to transfer to my chair, pump, and then transfer back into my car. At a as station one day, someone in a carload of older guys, who looked like they were heading out on a fishing trip, yelled, "Asshole," and then, "What kind of chump makes his woman pump his gas?"

I wanted to reply, "One who doesn't walk," or something to that effect. But the girl yelled something before I even had a chance to respond, as if she had to come to my defense. That made me feel disabled.

My friends started getting married, my twenties were over, and being out at the bars with friends all the time simply bored me. And then I met Elizabeth.

2

A compass is a device for determining directions by means of a magnetic needle pointing to the magnetic north, as opposed to true north. It is most often used to find one's way in the world, or just the woods while hiking or on water while boating.

Elizabeth

I met Andrew on New Year's Eve at the Millennium Ball held in Portsmouth, New Hampshire. All the talk was about the world ending and Y2K putting society into darkness with massive power outages and computer failures. I was finishing my dissertation on the role of reincarnation in modern-day literature for my PhD in English. I had been unsure that journalism, the subject of my undergrad degree, was what I wanted to keep doing, so why not return to school?

I would have been happy spending the New Year's holiday on my brown velour couch (this was back when I thought it was okay to pick up used furniture on street corners) in my new fleece pajamas, sent as part of my Christmas package from my parents, who were traveling on safari over the holidays. My plan was to order Chinese takeout and watch a variety of 1980s films, including *Footloose*, *Dirty Dancing*, and *The Breakfast Club*. Maybe I would be awake for the ball dropping and the world ending. Or maybe I would wake up in 2000 right where I left off: on the living room couch of the apartment I shared with three grad assistants: Jen, Rebecca, and Dori. They were headed out for the evening with friends, and I waved from the comfort of my pajamas.

Jen was finishing a big article on the history of karaoke for *New Hampshire Magazine*, so we roommates had spent the last few evenings at local karaoke hot spots around town, supporting her as she interviewed karaoke junkies. Jen had a real knack for helping people to express their innermost thoughts about a wide range of subjects, including but certainly not excluding tai chi, Olympic sport curling, World War II weapons, and the mating habits of the cuckoo bird. She also did some side work as an editor, calling her business "Writer's Ink," which we all agreed was incredibly clever. At some point in her past life, Jen had been a designer or banker; her attention to detail and ability to manage money exceeded anyone I knew.

Dori was a professional singer in a past life, I swear, because she gave the karaoke experts a good challenge. Her rendition of "Midnight Train to Georgia" brought a few customers to tears as they enjoyed their scorpion bowls or rum punch. However, she would say she had been reincarnated from a Spanish poet who lived in an artists' colony in the 1920s.

In the bars, Rebecca found interesting or intellectual men to chat with, often coming back to report that we had been invited to so-and-so's the next weekend for barbecue or a poetry reading. We all decided she must have been a biologist or wilderness explorer in a previous life, because she was a storehouse of trivia about the outdoors, like how many people had died on Mt. Washington over the centuries. With this knowledge, combined with her experience as a forest ranger in her undergrad years, she's the person I would want to be with me if I suddenly decided to hike the Appalachian Trail.

These girls kept me laughing and included me in social activities, but I was tired, and therefore more excited about the couch.

They had used every trick in the book to get me to change my mind:

"Only old ladies love velour couches."

"Takeout is fine when there aren't other perfectly acceptable options."

"Come on, our treat!"

"Did you get head lice again?"

"The eighties called, and they want their movies back."

I had laughed and thanked them all for their concern, and I promised I would be available for social activities tomorrow.

Around six that evening, as I was gathering my supplies for the weekend—Chinese takeout menu, onion dip and chips, hot chocolate, and waffles—another girlfriend, Kelly, called to say she desperately needed me to go with her to the Millennium Ball at Pease Air Force Base in Portsmouth, just up the road from the University of New Hampshire, where we were all graduate students. With Kelly, the request always began with "this handsome man"; this time, it was one she'd met downtown at a Veterans' fundraiser. He had chatted her up a while and invited her to be his guest at the ball, since it was New Year's, after all.

Initially, Kelly had turned him down, since it would be strange to attend a big, elegant affair with someone she hardly knew. But after talking with her mother—who was concerned that Kelly was thirty, unmarried, and with few "prospects" to make her a grandmother—Kelly decided to take the plunge and show up. She told me it was forty dollars per person, which was a lot of money to me for one night out, and I didn't drink much. But she couldn't show up alone, she said. And she added that there would probably be a hundred single men there. And it was New Year's and the millennium, so if the world ended, at least we would be together.

I hadn't been on a date since a pretentious real estate agent at the Brewery had asked why I hadn't dressed up more for a blind date—that is, according to my neighbors, who had set me up on that boring date. It didn't matter, because I had already decided my date was devoid of personality and would not get another opportunity to date me.

It had been a cold October night, the kind where temperatures are frigid enough for snow but precipitation still falls in liquid form. I had worn sensible jeans and boots with a stylish black turtleneck sweater and turquoise fleece, which Jennifer had told me looked great with my dark hair and green eyes. I also had an adorable aqua, yellow, and orange knit hat sans pom-pom.

So, as I sat on the couch, I took to heart Kelly's statement that my last date was back in October. And I decided to put my movie night on hold and wait for the world to end at the Millennium Ball with her by my side.

Always the quiet observer at these kinds of things, I knew my sole purpose was to arrive with Kelly so she didn't look alone and to hope that the single dude from the veterans fundraiser was there. I dragged out my last bridesmaid dress; there had been seven weddings the previous summer, and I had been a bridesmaid in five. This was the best black, ankle-length dress to be found. It could be dressed up with a fun necklace and dressed down with a sweater, scarf, or flip-flops. I opted to go conservative with sparkly earrings, not dangling, and a subtle necklace on the off chance I met someone interesting. It was, after all, New Year's Eve.

We spotted the "handsome man" immediately and learned his name was Scott. He greeted us with a friendly smile and made introductions to his friends. Only then did my eyes rest on the winning grin of his brother, the man who would become my husband.

3

True north is the North Pole, also known as geographic north. However, a compass does not point directly to true north due to Earth's tilt; it points to magnetic north.

Michelle

Being a lifeguard at a lake on rainy days gives me considerable time to think about random things. Today there are no little kids I have to watch carefully because their mothers are nose deep in a good book or busy having quality time with a husband, boyfriend, friend, etc. Bottom line, I'm horrified by some people's inability to pay attention to their kids near the water. Christ, I'm a kid, and I know better!

Other than that, lifeguarding is a great summer gig. It pays well, and I get good color, despite the SPF 50 my parents insist I use due to my fair skin and freckles. Senior year is starting in less than a month, and I'm excited about the soccer season and college right around the corner and maybe a boyfriend this year.

I love the story about how my parents met and fell in love, but I don't know how happy they are anymore. I mean, they pretend really well in public and show up together at our school events, unless Dad is traveling or not feeling well, which really means closing himself off in his bedroom. We all know he keeps a bottle of whisky behind the bookshelf of his man cave.

Pictures from back when they first met and when they were married and even when we were little are my favorites. The way Kelly tells the story about how quickly they fell in love is the best. Mom was planning to bring in the New Year on her couch, but Kelly needed her to be her wingman at this big ball she had been invited to. Practically dragged there against her will only because the world was about to end, Mom was only half listening—a skill she has perfected as a college professor—to Kelly and Scott flirt with one another when this "dashing" (who uses words like that?) man in a sporty wheelchair asked her to dance. She was unable to say no while processing how he could dance sitting down with a woman standing up, so he simply led her out on the floor, held her hands, and taught her how to move around his wheels to avoid squashing her toes.

I can see how Mom was caught off guard by Dad's confidence; he was a total ladies' man back then; I've seen the pictures. His hair has started to turn to a distinguished salt and pepper, my favorite euphemism for gray. My parents were old when they had us, not ancient or anything like that, but way older than my friends' parents, because it took so long for Mom to get pregnant as a result of Dad's injury.

My parents told us how we were conceived pretty much immediately after the birds-and-bees conversation, which was not so much a conversation as reading a pop-up book as a family. Bad idea. A pop-up book on how babies are made? Seriously! And why would they have the conversation with both my brother, Stephen, and me? We are close in age, but no boy or girl wants to hear that from both parents with a sibling seated alongside.

The following day, they sat us at the kitchen table to tell us we were test-tube babies. Parents can be so weird. Stephen closed his eyes and asked to be excused; he promptly left the table to play his saxophone loudly in his room. As the oldest, I needed to at least pretend to be interested, if only their sake. Mom explained that Dad had sperm but they couldn't get to where they were going without medical intervention. So doctors removed her eggs and his sperm, and mixed them all together and ended up with many embryos. During class, I told my teacher, Ms. Seidel, how some babies are made and then how we were made. I'm sure it made for awkward parent-teacher conferences that year.

I had always done well in school, but Stephen struggled more in elementary school. It wasn't that he couldn't read; he just opted out. Clearly, he's smart, but school isn't his thing. Luckily, I paved the way for him, and he always had teachers who nurtured the artsy, slightly quirky parts of him. We do agree that it is completely cool—miraculous, really—that we are even here, because if those doctors weren't geniuses, we wouldn't be. Fifty years ago, Dad wouldn't have been able to have his own children, but thanks to technology, here we are.

There is also tremendous pressure; because my parents wanted us extra bad, we can't disappoint them. Ms. Seidel told us then that Stephen and I must be old souls, that we've probably lived many times before this life. When I asked Mom and Dad about reincarnation, they told me to see if I could find things to read about it. Neither one had an opinion, but there is something comforting about the idea that we might be surrounded by the same people in each life we live.

I've always done the right thing, within reason, but lately that has gotten really boring. The other night, Courtney, my best friend since sixth grade, was driving us home from the movies in her white convertible Volkswagen Cabriolet. She said I ought to loosen up a bit, spend less time working and thinking about my classes. She lectured,

"It won't matter twenty years from now if we had an A in chemistry if we are never going to be chemists."

"Point taken," I replied, "but I'm a product of an established pattern of behavior."

"That's what I'm talking about, Michelle. Who seriously talks like that? What's with the 'established pattern of behavior' bullshit?"

I can remember the moon being out and the wind blowing our hair around and imagining that we must look like supermodels with fans on us. "Courtney, you have the balance all figured out. I do not," I argued while she cracked up. She spends all of her time talking about how we're going to really live it up this year because it's our last year of high school, and if we're going to screw up, this is the time to do it. I'm not one to screw up, but the idea of not being such a Goody Two-Shoes is very appealing. But look at me; I'm actually analyzing how I'm going to be more spontaneous.

"Don't think so much, Michelle; just enjoy the ride," she said. While I desperately wanted to believe her (along with my own ability to change), it seemed completely counterintuitive to the way I spent my first three years of high school preparing for college. I also spent ninth and tenth grade begging my parents to send me to private high school to give me more of chance to get into a competitive college. I'm a smart kid who works hard, and I'm involved in as many volunteer and extracurricular activities as I can possibly work into my schedule. But college professor mother claims, "Education achieved is based upon efforts exerted." So it doesn't matter where I learn what I need to learn as long as I learn it. Really, I would just like to be someplace bigger, with slightly more diversity—not necessarily racial diversity or even socioeconomic (love that word) diversity, but where kids come from different places.

At this point, though, I'm about to start my senior year and have accepted that there is no chance I'm dragging my parents back to the city now that they are so settled here in their careers. They love the idea of raising us in the mountains, and we've been lucky to grow up as skiers, hikers, and cyclists. But living here in Lincoln can be so boring, and the nearest mall is like a hundred miles from here. Well, not that far, but at least forty-five minutes away.

Stephen loves it here, so it's really three against one, which is unfair. He will be a junior, and he won't even notice I've left for college, since he's so wrapped up in his music. Dad is hardly home, and Mom hides behind whatever book she's reading, writing, or teaching from. I can't remember the last time my parents went out on a date or even carried on a normal conversation at the dinner table. Yes, my mother still forces us to eat dinner as a family, even when Dad is traveling. She claims this is how families stick together when the chaos of life seems overwhelming. My mother has a lot to say, but Dad is the talker in the family.

4

Magnetic north is the direction in which a compass needle points, at an angle from the direction of true north.

Stephen

I love my house. My family is okay, maybe not any more or less weird than anyone else's family, but I definitely love my house. It's comfortable, roomy, and I'm here a lot by myself. This way no one complains I'm playing my music too loud.

The first part of was built around the turn of the century—not this one, the one before. Then, over the years, different people built additions that make it look eccentric from the road. Like, if someone asked me to describe my house, I couldn't say, "It's the red Cape or Colonial or condo on the right," because its shape is unique. Instead, I say, "Turn down Pollard Road. Look for the large field on the left if you are headed north, and then there will be a red house. That's mine, Number Eleven, Pollard Road." And we have a mailbox, which is uncommon for our town, because almost everyone has post office boxes. I don't usually tell people about the mailbox, and I can't remember the last time I had to describe where I lived to anyone.

What is cool about my house is that my mother wrote the previous owner a letter when we were little and living in North Woodstock. In the letter, she told him how much she loved his house and that if he ever wanted to put it on the market, he should call her first. His wife had become disabled when she was older, so the last renovation made their home completely handicapped accessible, which is important for my dad, since he has been in a wheelchair my entire life.

When I was little, my dad couldn't fit through my bedroom door in the condo we lived in, and that always made me sad. So we read books on the couch or in my parents' bed, and it was a treat to fall asleep next to him. Then my mom would carry me upstairs, because that's where I always woke up.

A few years passed, and when the man was ready to move in with his daughter and her family, he called and sold his house to us for an amount my parents could afford when they sold our condo. So we moved into our first stand-alone house when I was seven and Michelle was eight.

Our house has a bunch of strange nooks and crannies due to the additions over the years. Both my parents have offices that are strange shapes. Mom's is a real office but on the smallish side, with an old school wooden desk housing her computer. The rest of the room feels like a tiny, eclectic book store filled with painted bookshelves holding an absurd amount of books and pictures of us. She is professor at Plymouth State University, fifteen miles south.

Dad's office doesn't look like an office but more like a man cave. In there he displays his World War II collection of helmets, books, uniforms, old guns—all dusty, of course, because he can't reach them all on the shelves. And Mom refuses to take care of that room—not because she's mean, but she always says Dad is a resourceful man, and if something is important to him, he will find a way. I suppose I could offer to do that for him when he's in a good mood.

He sometimes goes in there and closes the door. He doesn't want us to bother him when the door is closed, so we leave him alone. Michelle thinks he is in there boozing it up, but I'm not sure about that. He just likes his private time. He doesn't make scenes in public or anything like that, and he's always good to his family, so we don't make a big deal out of it. Drinking isn't a problem unless it negatively affects other people, and I don't feel negatively affected.

Tonight Dad and I are going to a movie. We haven't done that in a while, but we both love movies, and it's a way of doing something together where we don't actually have to talk. When Dad is out and about, he's everyone's best friend, and he drinks socially. He smiles a lot and can talk to anyone; my sister has that same quality. Michelle has a lot more friends than I do as a result, yet still doesn't like being at our school. My parents' friends know Dad is quieter at home.

Dad doesn't like to talk about how he was injured. Sometimes he will mention that car accident in the spring of his junior year of high school, but rarely. I know the story because Greg, a friend of my dad's from high school, isn't afraid to talk about it when he comes to visit. They actually became better friends after his accident. Dad pulled away from his closer group of pals after becoming paralyzed, and Greg treated him like a regular person, which Dad really appreciated. They played soccer together, and Greg went on to play at Northeastern University, where he became an architect. He now lives on Martha's Vineyard with his wife, Holly, and two daughters. We visit them sometimes in the summer, but Dad hates sand. He says it makes him feel like a battered shrimp. Michelle loves the ocean though, so we go only every couple of years.

Mom doesn't push him to talk about the accident. He was already paralyzed when they met, so why would it matter? I think it does matter, because I think he is still angry over what happened, how he lost his ability to use his legs, and everyone else in the accident was able to walk away. Dad had taken his girlfriend, Greta Hawthorne (she sounds famous, doesn't she?), as his date to the prom with Kevin, whom Greg claims was always an asshole, and Kevin's girlfriend, whose name I've never been told.

Dad has shown me pictures from that night, the last event he was able to stand up for. The pictures are old, for sure, and their outfits—costumes, really—are borderline ridiculous, but he looked tall and pretty well put together. Greta was truly stunning. She had that kind of impossible-to-recreate-with-chemicals, practically transparent blond hair, and eyes like small, strikingly blue planets. I can tell by his smile how proud he was to have a girl like that on his arm.

Dad is always quick to tell both Michelle and me that Greta was as smart and funny and kind as she was beautiful. She ended up going kind of far away to college, but I guess she and Dad kept in touch over the years. I think he tells me these things to get me to open up about girls, but I don't like to share too much there.

Dad wasn't a drinker in high school and always felt lucky that he was well liked enough that he didn't feel pressure to drink or use drugs to fit in with any one crowd. I wish I had inherited that from him. I wish I could feel what it's like to be happy in my own skin. I wish I could look at a beautiful girl who also happens to be smart, funny, and nice, and hope that maybe she would like to stand next me. Dad probably thinks it's weird I don't bring girls home to meet my family or groups of guys by the house for pick-up soccer in our side yard, which houses a soccer goal.

The night Dad was hurt, he was being a regular teenager on his way home from the prom. Apparently, they were goofing around while Dad was driving. The police said that he wasn't under the influence or speeding. The roads were somewhat wet, so that could have contributed to his losing control of the car and crashing into the big elm tree near the center of town. No one who was with him that night, including the three other people, said anything odd led to the loss of control.

Dad was popular before and after his accident. I wouldn't consider myself to be popular, but I'm certainly not a complete social outcast. I'm one of those guys who flies just under the radar, not so quirky that I'm bullied, but also not really anything worth noticing either. Dad probably wishes I would be more competitive, since I played soccer and skied and rode bikes all the time as a kid. People say I'm handsome like Dad, but I don't own a room like he does. I'm about to be a junior in high school, and really the only thing I care about besides my family is my music.

5

This difference of angle when looking at a map is called
declination, *or more specifically, according to Merriam again,*
"The angular distance north or south from the celestial equator
measured along a great circle passing through the celestial poles."
Interestingly, it also means "a turning aside or swerving."

Jessie

Allison and I met on a blind date, one of the most awkward dates I've ever been on. My old friend from elementary school, Cathy, a teacher who happens to work at the same school as Allison's sister, Jill, was more nervous than either of us. Between the two women who set us up, Allison and I could not get a word in edgewise, but we were interested enough to want to see each other again.

Cathy and Jill stood up with us two years later, when we were married in front of our closest friends and family in a civil ceremony; we wore white linen pantsuits.

We both wanted children, especially coming from large families, but Allison is ten years older than me, so we weren't sure if we should use one of her eggs and a sperm donor, with me as the carrier. The process turned out to be far more complicated than we could imagine, but between our two salaries, mine as a graphic designer and hers as a veterinarian, we were able to swing the costly procedures at Dartmouth Hitchcock Medical Center. In retrospect, a Boston clinic would have been closer to Portsmouth, and easier maybe, but as a teenager, I had been treated at Dartmouth and always been taken good care of. Plus, I needed any excuse to get back to the mountains of my childhood. Allison loves to hike and bike and ski as well, which makes her the favorite spouse amid my parents' five adult children.

Long story short, we live in an old Victorian on Middle Road in Portsmouth, a great location for my office, since we're so busy. Allison's vet clinic is just down Interstate 95 in Newburyport, about a twenty-minute drive, depending on traffic. My work allows me the flexibility to be the primary taxi driver for the kids' many activities. Having twins as babies was wild, and we had been lucky to have the help of our parents and nearby siblings. Now that Brian and Caroline are in ninth grade, they're getting closer to becoming rational human beings. Many of our friends are getting ready to retire, and we're working on putting money away for college, which will be here before we know it.

Fourteen years have flown by, and the kids seem to be doing okay with our untraditional family of four. Society still challenges us for being lesbians and wanting to be mothers. But Brian and Caroline have plenty of positive males role models between my two brothers and Allison's three brothers, and we are sure to check in with the school to make sure other kids are treating them well. It's helped that they have grown up here in Portsmouth, so their friends have grown up with the fact that Brian and Caroline have two mommies.

When they were little, they called me "Mommy" and Allison "Momma," which worked well, until, say age ten or so, when Mommy/Momma suddenly was juvenile, according to Caroline. Brian continued to call us that for a brief period, just to tease his sister, but it's been shortened to the collective "Moms." If we're in public and they can't get our attention, they resort to calling us by our first names, which is what most teenagers do if no one is responding quickly enough. They also use MJ or MA (pronounced Maw), which I have liked now that they are teenagers. We're fine with this, as it rolls off the tongue easily enough.

Before they were born, we spent hours talking about what they would call us. I have friends from college who adopted, and their kids called them "Mom and Jane." Weird, right? Mom and Mommy or Ma were other options, but in the end, it didn't matter what we wanted them to call us; they figured out what they needed to call us. Allison's dad, who desperately wanted to be called Grandpa, was called only PeePaw until Caroline turned three. I know she did it to drive him crazy. No one would ever tell her what she could or couldn't do. That independent streak has always been very visible.

People have teased us over the years about how Caroline shares our traits, despite not being biologically ours. Certainly things like independence and stubbornness are on both sides of our family trees, but Caroline is also uniquely individual. She didn't laugh as much as most children, but we've always thought her to be happy. She attended kids' birthday parties and participated in everything, but I'm not sure how much she enjoyed those social outings.

She was also interested in learning about religion so we took turns taking her to different churches in the area. Some weekends we were Congregationalists, while others we were Episcopalian or Methodists. All were welcoming to our family. But, when Caroline was about eleven, maybe ten, she heard that the local Catholic church had a CYO basketball league, which had games on Friday nights. That schedule didn't interfere with her skiing on weekends, while the local recreation department had games on Saturday mornings. So, she asked if she could start going to the Catholic church regularly in the fall with our neighbors, whose children were all grown.

When Caroline approached Father Dan to sign up for the league, he told her that the league was actually only for boys, but that she could participate by being on the pep squad. Tony, our neighbor, tells what happened next perfectly: she thanked him for his time, but she would not be cheering for anyone else; if someone wanted to cheer for her, though, that would be fine, and she was no longer Catholic. No one had the heart to inform her that she technically wasn't actually Catholic. She promptly left the church to wait for Tony and Polly outside.

Father Dan gave us a call later that day to see that she was all right and to explain that he was saddened by her abbreviated foray into the Catholic faith, and that she would always be welcomed back. It was only a matter of days before she announced to her fifth-grade class that she had denounced Catholicism, and others would be wise to follow suit.

Then we received a call from her teacher to tell us that she was using this as a way of isolating herself from the other children. I remembered saying something like "Well, this is a public school; certainly, not every kid there is a devout Catholic."

Ms. Steeves replied, "No, Catholics are in a minority here, but kids are sometimes annoyed by other kids who have such headstrong beliefs this early in life."

I tried to explain that Caroline's soul was an old one and that she had not always thought like most kids. Ms. Steeves agreed and promised to speak with her about toning it down a little bit—never to compromise her beliefs, but to keep some of them on the low burner and to use the home environment to build her defense strategy.

6

A switchback is a hiking term used to describe the process of zigzagging up a steep incline as opposed to walking straight up. This makes the incline more manageable.

Allison

I wanted to give up my practice as a veterinarian to homeschool our children when they were ready for public kindergarten. I was too worried about how other children would treat them, even at the bus stop. Some kids are mean, and though I came from a "normal" family, I have terrible memories of having to run through the woods to avoid neighborhood bullies. What could possibly happen to our little guys? They have been at risk ever since we allowed ourselves to dream that we could be parents after all.

After a number of different scans and blood tests, doctors had told me my eggs were too old. And Jessie had a lot of scar tissue around her ovaries and a strangely shaped uterus, which we learned made getting pregnant very difficult, even through in utero or in vitro fertilization. We were advised to adopt embryos as opposed to going through both an egg and a sperm donor search. Embryos are sometimes frozen after a couple is finished creating their family. With the right conditions, a couple's embryos could become our children; they were our own potential for life.

We spent hours poring over binders full of possible donor parents, looking for the right combination of education, mental health, and wellness. We didn't care what physical features our children would have because, obviously, by of the sheer nature of us not being able to reproduce on our own, one of us would be left out. Oddly enough, Brian looks a little like Jessie's side of the family, and Caroline definitely favors mine, with her lighter hair, freckles, and green eyes. Brian's almost black hair and brown eyes often leave people questioning their twin relationship.

Our fertility team "defrosted" three embryos the first round and implanted the best growing two. When that time failed to result in a pregnancy, they "defrosted" four embryos for the second round. This left us down to our last three frozen embryos from the ten we adopted. We agreed that if this time didn't work, we would try to adopt a child rather than continue to spend thousands of dollars trying for a pregnancy. There were hundreds of kids in New Hampshire needing a good home, and I was happy to adopt. However, Jessie was weirded out by adopting. "Too many unknowns," she always said, though we'd chosen our embryos based on little more than the fact that the couple had wanted to help another family have children. And talk about unknown!

We decided on a donor: the mom was a professor, and the dad was disabled, and we knew from their application that they loved to be outside and actively participating in life. One of their children was blond and blue-eyed and the other brunette and brown-eyed; yet this had little bearing on what our children ultimately would look like. I learned not to argue over this, especially since the result would be actual children in any case.

There were some advantages to us not having our own genetic offspring, especially because there are some serious mental health problems on my side of the family. That doesn't mean we would be destined to have a child born with depression or anxiety or personality disorder. But my brother was diagnosed with schizophrenia when he was seventeen, and it put a tremendous strain on my parents. Just when he started to feel better, he would stop taking his medication and fall into a bad place. This cycle meant Mom and Dad were forever moving him in and out of halfway houses, hospitals, and shelters. Name it, and he lived in one at one point or another somewhere in Vermont.

All we had left were our last-chance embryos. Third time was the charm, and we ended up with Brian and Caroline. As their personalities started to develop, I breathed a sigh of relief when they made eye contact and smiled. These were physical affirmations that they would be less likely to have cognitive delays, speech problems, or autistic tendencies; they would be regular kids leading regular lives.

Even as a toddler, Brian was the optimist, the one living in the moment, taking every opportunity to make a memory. Little issues didn't frustrate him, and we worried he might be a pushover, since he rarely fought with his sister. I remember him saying at five or six years old, "Well, Caroline must need it more than me right now." He had a far better perspective on life than either Jessie or me. When he was in sixth or seventh grade, a teacher told him about Henry David Thoreau leaving his life and all of society to find simplicity in nature. He said to Jessie one night across the dinner table, "Can we go find his cabin on Walden Pond? It's educational, since Henry was a transcendentalist."

Pretending to look up something else on the computer, we quickly googled "transcendentalist," since neither one of us was an English major or had any interest in that period of history. We decided it would be a fun family field getaway, so we scheduled a trip to Lexington and Concord. For weeks, it seemed, Brian would come home with some new fun fact about Henry David Thoreau. "Moms, did you know that Henry wanted to suck the marrow from his life? Do you know what that meant? It meant that when he came to the end of his life, he did not want to discover that he hadn't lived. He was really smart. Moms, did you know that?" What we did know was that we were getting our money's worth out of Mrs. Nelson that year.

The weekend of Walden Pond arrived, and ten-year-old Caroline was more than slightly irritated to be brought along, because she had "other things going on." I'm not sure what her plans included, but we thought she would like the trip. After we parked in the small lot next to the re-creation of Thoreau's cabin, Caroline asked, "What is that awful smell?" Then, "Is that a highway over there?" Later, a tour guide for the Thoreau Lyceum told the kids a waste treatment plant was right down the street. Caroline's response was something like "Oh, that's nice. Way to keep the memory of the world-class transcendentalist alive by letting a dump and a highway be built close by."

Brian responded, "Well, Caroline, I'm sure this was beautiful when Thoreau was here, and who knows, it could be beautiful here again one day," as if his ten-year-old mind could see into the future.

None of us will forget our day at Walden Pond. As Brian had us take pictures of him pretending to carry armloads of wood from the trees to the little cabin, as Thoreau would have done, I thought, *Whoever gets this kid in class as a teenager will always be entertained; there is no doubt of that.*

7

*Blaze: A trail marker. May be in the form of colored tape,
bark chipped in a pattern from a tree and painted, etc.*

Brian

I've always sort of felt like this is just one life in many that I have
lived and will live again, so the fact that I have two mothers instead
of a mother and a father is not a big deal. My sister, Caroline, on the
other hand, makes it a big deal. If she would just relax and not worry
so much about what other people thought about her, she would be a
way happier person. I worry about her intensity and the fact that she
doesn't have as many friends as I do. She always wants to be alone,
even when it comes to sports, which she's really good at. She's also
constantly fighting with both of our parents over stuff that doesn't
even make sense.

   I read her diary once because one of my friends stole his
sister's, and we read it at lunchtime. Hers was interesting, but my
sister's read more like an exercise log and book tracker. It wasn't
worth sharing with anyone, so I put it back. There truly was not
one thing I could even tease her about, so what was the point? She
is supercompetitive in everything—grades, tennis, ski racing, and
downhill mountain biking.

   We honestly could not be more different. When we were
younger, people always asked on the twin thing; for example, could

we read each other's minds, complete each other's sentences? What they didn't understand—unless they became friends with our family, because why would we share all this private information with the world—is that we weren't meant to be twins; the only thing we shared is the womb.

By definition, twin-ship occurs when two eggs are released by the mother in the knick of time for the sperm to fertilize both eggs. Sometimes it's one egg that splits into two, as in the case of identical twins; but in most cases, twins begin as two different eggs. I learned this in fifth grade, technically, but my moms did a decent good job of always talking to us from an early age about how we happened a family.

Here is where we get interesting. Obviously, my moms couldn't produce a child on their own, nor did they choose to have a one-night stand with some guy just to get pregnant. Instead, they had someone else's embryos, three of them, implanted into Mom's (also known as Jessie's) uterus. (I've heard the story a thousand times. It's totally weird and not something I brag about publicly.) Therefore, we were not supposed to be twins, because we had been fertilized outside the uterus by two different sperm. But the conditions were such that we decided—well, it wasn't really much of a decision; I guess *stuck* is a better word. We stuck in Mom's uterine lining and were born "twins" only because there were two of us seven and a half months later. Yes, we were premature by almost two months, which I think explains why Caroline is so crazy competitive. I must have been getting all the good nutrients, and she was just trying to stay alive.

We were considered high risk because Mom had an oddly shaped uterus, so she was on bed rest forever, or so she makes it sound every time she tries to make us feel guilty about something we were supposed to do and didn't do. Most of the time, we are their miracle babies, especially because we were sick a lot as infants, and then they were so afraid of everyone else's germs, they didn't want us going to childcare outside the home, blah, blah, blah. That has probably spoiled us more than anything.

Despite all that, I'm almost six feet and still growing, so clearly the whole being born early thing didn't affect me much. I like to consider myself a Renaissance man: good at many things, but not into specializing. I play soccer and ski to keep the girls interested, but I'm really into the school's drama and improv comedy club. Making people laugh is entertaining, but I need to go to college so I at least have something to fall back on. Plus, the student government thing is cool too, since it forces people to have to listen to whatever soapbox I'm interested in.

However, I can't help but think from time to time about where I came from—especially when the extended family gets together and I forget my legacy is not tied up with their history. Like when Gram, Mom Ally's mom, was killed in that car accident last summer, there were so many people who forgot we weren't genetically linked to her. They would say things like "You have that sarcasm like your grandmother had" or "You have that uncanny ability like your grandmother to see right through people."

When we were cleaning out her home, the one she had raised my mom and her four siblings in, we found an ancient cookbook that had been my great-grandmother's. However, Gram didn't use it as a cookbook; she wrote poems in the margins, along with the birthdays and sometimes death dates of her children. (Back then, the mortality rate for babies was a lot higher, and she lost three children.)

Sadly, Gram's mom died when Gram was only six months old. The story was she had breast cancer, and doctors tried to perform a double mastectomy. She developed an infection and died. Crazy story, right? It's no wonder Gram was sarcastic and ornery on most days. She didn't have her ma close by when she was a baby, and her father was a bit of a bastard, from what I've gathered. Caroline, who is a bookworm and journal writer, said to me, "That's cool about Gram's mom using a cookbook to write poetry. Maybe that's where I get my love of books from."

"Except for the fact that we have no blood relation to her," I gently reminded her, and I can't help but think I've disappointed her with the truth. It's not like someone put us up as babies to have a better life. We weren't even babies yet, but Moms adopted us anyway and just hoped and prayed really hard. We found our way to them, and here we are.

8

Orienteering: *Using a map and a compass to navigate between points along an unfamiliar course.*

Caroline

First day of freshmen year, the note on my locker burned a hole in my backpack as I left the school parking lot after tennis practice. "You are a dyke too." People think that because this is *modern* society and we live in a fairly liberal community, nasty teenaged homophobes don't exist anymore —but they do. I don't understand how we can live in such a progressive, well-educated area, and yet I still have to attend school with ignorant little pissants. *Pissants* is a word my grandmother would use that makes me feel less angry.

Seriously, I'm the second-best singles player on our team, even as a freshman, and those girls still treat me like this. It has to be someone on the team, because no one else has access to the locker room, unless Coach unlocked it during practice for someone to use the bathroom. There have been too many vandalism incidents and bullying situations like this one, so that even our nice school is in lockdown mode all the time. I can't talk about this with Moms, or they will go barreling into the school again, like they did in middle school, and that just made it worse.

Maybe Brian has an idea about how to handle them. No one ever seems to bother him, which I don't understand, because he doesn't even care about being popular. He just always has friends. He likes to be the center of attention, something I can't stand, which is strange for someone who loves individual sports as much as I do. When I'm playing tennis or ski racing or flying down a mountain on my bike, I don't think about anything; I just move in a forward direction and turn or react or swing when my body tells me to. My coaches tell me this makes me a natural athlete and that I'm definitely college material for at least tennis and skiing, probably not so much for biking. My workouts keep me in shape for other things, but lately I've been feeling tired more than usual. It's probably just the high school level of competition I'm adjusting to.

Sports are something we've always done as a family, and I don't have to talk to anyone if I'm involved in a game, match, or ride. The conversations can't go very deep on a chairlift, and that's probably a relief to Moms; they can't possibly get into an argument with me, but it's still considered quality time.

They are both very active still, despite their ages. They were so worried about being old mothers when they were trying to get pregnant. They love each other, so I'm not annoyed by the fact that they're gay. They've given us everything we could ever want and more. It's the rest of the world that takes issue and that makes my life miserable in many ways. I wish it didn't. I wish I didn't resent my moms for a lifestyle I know they would not choose. I just wish my life could be easier. I wish friends wanted to come over for sleepovers. I wish I had friends period.

Don't get me wrong; there are girls in my classes who talk to me, who are polite and sit with me at lunch and we talk, but we have superficial conversations, as if everyone is afraid to get to know me too well. The word *superficial* has a negative connotation to it, and I don't mean to say those conversations are always bad. Even small talk keeps people connected. I just don't like to go into a long discussion about every issue out there in the world. Even the few girls from elementary school who weren't bugged by Moms being together now seem weirded out by it. I want to scream, "At least my parents love each other." And at least they come to my matches and my races and cheer me on, even when I'm generally a bitch at home.

That's the primary reason my best friends are books. When I'm not training, I'm reading, mostly squirreled away in my room. The door is mostly open, in case Brian or one of my moms wants to pop in. I like talking to them, but I'll never feel comfortable talking in front of class or having a lot of friends. One friend would be good though. Just one. Forget having a boyfriend. That would just be too much of a distraction from my sports. I need to stay focused.

9

Andrew

When we called Dartmouth about six months after donating our remaining embryos, we learned that ours had been adopted. Due to the anonymity of everything we had signed, we could never learn anything about the people, but I wanted to believe they were a friendly, professional man and woman who met and fell in love in college and couldn't get pregnant. I didn't want to know anything about how the children were being raised or where they lived, but it was reassuring that our "leftover" potential for life could make another family complete. I didn't think about them becoming children after that and was just grateful that they had been chosen and not left out there in a kind of frozen purgatory. Must be a man thing—the need to populate the earth—and that nothing in our social worker's "embryo adoption binder" made us look inferior or incapable of creating strong little people simply because of a spinal cord injury.

This is an area I'm still hung up on since my spinal cord injury. It was the worst part of being injured, even as a seventeen-year-old. I remember knowing that I would be okay, but I stressed about whether I would ever be able to parent a child. My dad and I were close, and I wanted that relationship with my own biological children.

Wheeling from one room to another in this old, rambling house of ours, I'm reminded of my disability daily. I feel like I've been a good father and husband, despite being gone a lot for work. I do want my children to love me, though Elizabeth might argue this fact. Michelle is a lot like me, and we get along well as far as fathers and daughters go. We probably trust her too much, because she hasn't ever gotten in trouble, but I did notice the other night that the door on my liquor cabinet was ajar. Stephen wouldn't dare, and Elizabeth drinks only wine, and that's rare these days, since she's been working so much. So it looks like I need to have a sit-down conversation with my only daughter about drinking and whatever else she might be up to.

Suddenly, she is a young woman wearing bikinis and flouncing around the house with her friends in their bikinis, and they have no idea how beautiful they are and that they must be driving the boys in their school crazy. She has always been a good kid, has worked hard in school, and thankfully has never been boy crazy. I'm afraid she realizes the attention boys will be paying to her now that she is a fully developed female and how very uncomfortable this makes me as her father. It was so much easier when she was eight, and we could just go fishing or swimming out on Squam Lake.

She has such a sense of compassion, one I lacked when I was her age. She volunteers, for God's sake, teaching kids with cognitive disabilities how to ski and snowboard. I remember being that age, a senior in high school, ready to take on the world. I also remember what seventeen-year-old boys are like. They are guided by one primary principle. And if they can't find it with Michelle, they will move on to another girl who will be more obliging. But I'm not really worried about Stephen pushing himself on girls. He

36

still seems very introverted, more in tune with his music than with asking someone out.

Elizabeth needs to be in on my conversation with Michelle. Maybe she's already on it, and I'm the one who's a chapter or two behind. I feel like we were just celebrating Michelle's first birthday, and now I'm going to have the awkward "Stay away from boys—don't let them in your pants—no one wants to date a whore—marry someone with a baby she had in high school" conversation again. Didn't we just have this conversation when she was in eighth grade? Where is Elizabeth?

10

Elizabeth

There are just some things we don't tell each other, because we know what the other handles well and not so well. The certified letter we received from Dartmouth will put Andrew over the edge. He never wanted to know anything about what happened with the embryos we put up for adoption almost sixteen years ago, so I never told him about the pregnancy that resulted in twins. Nurse Jolene said we could call her six months later to see if the embryo adoption led to a pregnancy, so I called then to learn that twins were born. I needed as much information as would be allowed legally to help protect Michelle and Stephen from falling in love with someone who was a full sibling. Like as parents we can even begin to think that we can protect our children from anything these days! So now I'm armed with their ages and the fact that they're twins born with assistance from the fertility clinic at Dartmouth Hitchcock Medical Center.

However, this letter is not what I expected. Now, not only do I have to tell Andrew that births occurred from our embryos, but that the adoption parents have requested our help and are desperate to learn our identity. One of their children, our biological offspring, is sick with pediatric acute leukemia and could be helped with a bone marrow transplant if a donor match could be found.

This has been a fear and a hope of mine ever since Michelle and Stephen reached school age. Not that another child would be sick—no, of course not—I would never wish that on any mother. I have often wondered about these children, not because I would want to parent them, but more about what they're like, what they're interested in. Do they look like Stephen or Michelle as babies? Are they happy, chatty children or quiet and introverted like me? If we could do anything to help, we would in an instant.

When I called Dartmouth to speak with Nurse Jolene, I asked her what kind of family we were talking about, just so I could prepare Andrew. She told me that, due to the anonymity clause, she could not disclose that information.

I may be accused of overanalyzing my husband's character, but one flaw is his refusal to discuss alternative lifestyles. Though he has always been a professional and a loving, well-mannered, and respectful husband, my fear has been how his homophobia will rub off on our kids. Am I not giving him enough credit? He would still do anything to help anyone in his family, even if they are unknown to him. Delivery of this information will be essential in how we move on, but time is of the essence if we are going to help this young person. The child is only two years younger than Stephen, and I can't imagine the despair and helplessness the parents must be feeling.

We have our own mess going on with the two teenagers we are raising right now, so Andrew has no right to be judgmental of the way another family is living their life. Stephen's guidance counselor called the other day to discuss his dropping grades, even in band, his absolute favorite class. I feel like a failure as a parent, since I didn't look at his progress report that came out two weeks ago.

Michelle is a train wreck too right now, only a different kind of mess. I haven't told Andrew about that either. When he gets back from Boston, we need to sit down and talk about how we are going to handle this first major adolescent debacle. Courtney's mom, Rina, called me last night at ten to come pick up Michelle after her husband, Mike, had to drag her out of the woods behind their house on a tarp, too drunk to walk and too heavy to carry. How embarrassing.

Michelle told me she was sleeping over at Courtney's house, as they have been friends since middle school, and she'd never given me any reason not to trust her. But somehow I knew this time would be different. Apparently, a few friends had a little party out in the woods, and when Michelle passed out, Courtney panicked and ran to her house to get help, which is exactly what she should have done in that situation.

I left Andrew a message saying that we needed to talk and have dinner out tomorrow night. I would meet him in Concord at Moritomo's so we could establish a strategy together, and I would also have to let him know about the Friday meeting I set up with the social worker through Dartmouth Hospital regarding the embryo adoption. Won't he love me then?

11

Michelle

There's nothing more humiliating than waking up naked next to my mother, in *her* bed, mind you, with twigs, leaves, and the remnants of dried vomit in my hair. I will never be able to face Courtney's parents again after her dad had to drag me out of their woods because I passed out too far away to carry home. Seriously, I hadn't had that much to drink, I thought, but maybe it was the combination of the seven different kinds of alcohol, plus the fact that none of us ate dinner. Ugh.

Mom made me go to work this morning too, and I told my boss I had a stomach bug. When he called my mother to come pick me up, she informed him that I needed to finish my shift. I'm surprised she didn't tell him I had to be dragged out of the woods on a tarp by my friend's dad. For being quiet and reserved most of the time, she is fairly badass when it comes to holding us to task. I'm surprised she didn't also tell him to fire me. The smell of eggs, bacon, pancakes, and everything—even the coffee I poured for people—just about put me over the edge all morning.

If Courtney hadn't freaked out, we would have been fine, but now I'm practically on lockdown for the rest of the fall. There's even talk of not being able to drive a car until Christmas because of my irresponsibility. Mom needs time to "process" and talk to Dad about the next steps. Process my ass. She's just pissed that she has to pay more attention to us right now.

They have it good with Stephen and me; although I'm not sure how happy Stephen is right now, since he hardly comes out of his room, except to eat three peanut butter and jelly sandwiches for lunch. I guess there's no need to worry unless he stops eating altogether. It's really their fault, raising us to be independent. Mom is angry because this makes her look like a bad parent, and Dad doesn't even know about it yet, since he's traveling. He has no room to argue, because he drinks in his man cave every night, and it's only because he's in a wheelchair that he doesn't make a scene when he drinks too much. That probably isn't fair, but neither is the fact that this is the first time I've really screwed up in my entire adolescence.

There must be something else going on, because Mom was all jumpy this afternoon when I was looking through the crap on the table for my fall soccer schedule. She scooped up some paperwork and took it to her office, which is off-limits to us, unless I need to borrow a book or something. I really wish she would take a yoga class to relax or meet up with some friends to go out to dinner or take in a movie. Christ, Dad gets out and has friends. Maybe they should do something together. But God forbid I suggest we do something as a family.

I wonder how dysfunctional our family is compared to other people's. I mean, at least my parents are still married, and we appear functional on the outside. Well, we did until I was dragged out of the woods on a blue tarp.

Courtney thought we should just stick to beer for our first time drinking together, to be on the safe side, but I thought Dad wouldn't notice if we just took a little off the top of each of his bottles in the cabinet. Dumb in retrospect. It won't happen again, since I can't afford to get arrested during soccer. I'd miss the rest of my senior season, especially since I'm the captain; that would look really bad.

Kids are bound to make mistakes, and if this is one of the few times I make my parents look uninformed, they'll get over it. Nobody is dead, after all.

12

Stephen

Lately, I've been leaving school for lunch at home. Now that I'm a junior, I get to have "release," which allows me to head home at lunchtime for a mere twenty-five minutes, but it's a decent break in the day. Michelle takes her release with her friends Courtney or Sarah, and they just eat their sandwiches outside somewhere. Her friends are embarrassing.

Most brothers would be psyched if their sister had all of her hot friends over to the house, but I just can't stand it when they're over. They try to make me talk. One time in middle school, I came home from my friend Mike's house, and her whole soccer team was skinny-dipping in our backyard, which although private from the road was certainly not private from me. Dad was away, and Mom thought I was sleeping over at Mike's. She didn't think it was a big deal, but it may have scarred me for life.

So, I whipped up three peanut butter sandwiches on wheat bread and sat down at the kitchen table. I read the letter from the hospital that Mom put on her desk after she finished yelling at Michelle for what I'm now calling "the blue tarp incident." My progress report had been somewhere in the pile of crap on her desk and had gone unnoticed or uncommented on for at least a week, so I was just going to put it toward the top when the words "PLEASE

CONTACT US IMMEDIATELY AS TIME IS OF THE ESSENCE" caught my eye. So, I read the paragraph below, which said a person needed to see if any of my family members were a genetic match for a bone marrow transplant.

What could they possibly want with our bone marrow? And why ours? It doesn't make sense that a hospital would send out random letters to people, though I've heard of bone marrow drives. Unless it's someone related to us, but then wouldn't they just ask us directly? Seems weird to have a hospital send the request through a social worker, which is who signed the letter.

I like to help people. I knew I could just give them a call, use my deepest phone voice, and pretend to be Andrew Walker. Dad often makes jokes when he meets people for the first time by shaking someone's hand and introducing himself: "I'm Andrew Walker, good to meet you. Well, I used to be a walker; now I just rock and roll," and then he does a little wheelie in his chair. He claims it puts people at ease with the whole wheelchair thing. So, if he can do it, I can do it. I'm a junior in high school, practically a full-grown man.

I dialed, cleared my throat, and asked to speak with the social worker, Casey Chase. I wasn't sure if a man or a woman would pick up. "Casey Chase, how can I help you?" *Clearly a man*, I observed.

I told him, "This is Andrew Walker," and he very loudly thanked me for responding to the letter so quickly, then explained that they really didn't like to use certified mail but, legally, it was required. The fact that he was believing I was a middle-aged man was fantastic.

He asked if I understood the reason for his call, and instead of keeping it brief and simply replying, "Not exactly," I launched into an awkward string of wordiness, which sounded a little like "Aware of bone marrow drives certainly but not sure about what you need exactly from me so no, not exactly." Casey elaborated by first stating that he understood that I was aware of the embryo adoption that took place about fifteen years ago. I was thinking, *What is he talking about?* But because I was acting as confident, adult Andrew Walker, I responded, "Yes, of course."

"There has been a request for the anonymity clause to be lifted, so that the adopted parents can contact you directly regarding a medical emergency." I said nothing. Crickets on the other end of the phone—my end, that is. Casey kept talking. "I have permission to share that the couple who adopted all ten of the embryos had a set of twins, and one is now suffering from pediatric acute lymphocytic leukemia." Good Lord. Sweet Jesus. Holy Mary, mother of God. I felt as if a now-deceased grandparent were speaking through me, and all I could think was *This is interesting information.*

"Yes, this does sound like an emergency," I said. "And I'm sure my par—I'm sure my wife and children would want to help if we are able. Lift the clause, and send us the information we need."

"Yes, certainly, and can I have an updated address? Apparently, Lincoln is a small enough that the postmaster knew where to find your family despite having changed addresses years ago. We will need both you and your wife to sign the anonymity clause and fax it back to us. Do you have a fax?"

Why would we have a fax machine? "Tell you what, Casey, why don't you just fax it to my kids' school, and I'll grab it from there this afternoon." I knew Ms. Hollos in guidance would be fine with that. I provided him the fax number, which I had recently memorized, thanks to applying for various music electives online, and I gave him our address. "I will need to speak to Mom—I mean, my wife, Elizabeth, but please send our information to whoever needs it.

Thank you for the information. If I have any questions, may I direct my call to you?"

Casey gave me his direct line as I scrambled for paper and a pen and decided to use the back of my shitty progress report. He thanked me for the opportunity to help another family and said he was happy I was home, making some comment about how people are so busy they don't always respond to messages anymore, especially old-fashioned ones like his, which require an actual conversation. Casey sounded like he was probably good at helping people when they needed it. I mentally made a note to become a social worker if my music career doesn't work out long term.

"Have a wonderful day," I told him in the booming voice the real Andrew Walker would use.

13

Jessie

Returning to Portsmouth Hospital for her follow-up appointment last night was stressful enough; I was a wreck. Caroline had been hiding out in her room at night for weeks, but we assumed she was just tired from classes starting and from the fall tennis schedule working her over. Always a serious competitor, she was not one to complain about fatigue or muscle soreness, but we were noticing that she was often popping a few ibuprofen here and there. She had just had her high school physical in July, but they don't do blood work anymore unless there's a reason.

Brian's appointment had been right before hers, so the pediatrician was still cracking up over how animated, high-energy, and chatty he was, so I thought Caroline was just being quiet. She neglected to mention feeling tired, having headaches, dealing with joint stiffness, etc. Dr. Lakey did question the bruising on her legs, and Caroline chalked it up to some summer hiking incidents and working at day camp.

She had always been the kind of kid who popped up out of bed in the morning, not chatty like her brother, but wasting no time in getting ready for school, work, or whatever was on her plan for the day. We didn't have to remind her to eat a healthy breakfast, as she had been preparing her own scrambled eggs and fruit smoothies since she turned twelve, sometimes even making them for the rest of the family. Brian still lived on cereal and a banana. We consciously tried not to compare the two of them, but, with twins, it's often difficult not to.

However, before those first few days of school, I had to wake her up in the morning, which was unheard of. We grew worried and thought maybe she had developed anemia. I called Dr. Lakey about getting her back in for a follow-up appointment, wondering aloud if they ought to order more tests. Caroline didn't want to be taken out of school for her appointment; nor did she want to miss tennis. Fortunately, we were able to squeeze her into the last slot, 4:45, so she had to leave practice only a few minutes early.

The nurse took a blood sample and sent it off to the lab, and Dr. Lakey interrogated Caroline more closely about her body. Only then did she disclose how frequently she had been taking vitamin I, as Brian calls it (ibuprofen). She had been experiencing discomfort in her shoulders, neck, and elbows but had explained away the pain as athletic in nature: sore muscles from intense practicing. The headaches had been harder to explain, but she thought they were from stress induced by school.

I looked at her in that moment with questioning eyes, as she had not mentioned this to me at all. Clearly, she did not want to elaborate in front of me either. This concerned me because, although quiet, our daughter was more in tune with her body and how it worked most efficiently than anyone else her age, or even my age. I worried this was far more serious than anemia or fatigue. Why hadn't she mentioned this to us sooner? The fact she was mentioning it now must mean that she was worried as well, a big burden for a little girl, even if she was the number-one tennis player in the state. I reached over to hold her hand, but she pulled it away and slipped it into the front pocket of her hoodie.

When I was pregnant, Rob, a friend of mine from college, lost his six-year-old son in a car accident. An elderly woman driver never even slowed down as she approached the crosswalk. Rob believed the driver clearly had time to see them, slow down, and stop. Not only had Rob been watching his eldest son in the crosswalk with his bike, he was pulling his two-year-old son in the tow-behind bike trailer, so he had also seen the accident.

I remember the funeral, the hundreds of people who flocked to the church to say good-bye to a little boy who had truly packed more in six years than many of us do in a lifetime. The heat was unbearable as I grieved for my friend, his wife, and his little girl, and for the little boy who never got to grow up. When I hugged Rob, he put his hands on my expanding belly, and whispered, "Take care of those babies." Even on a good day, I'm reduced to tears when I think about that moment fifteen years ago in our friendship. We do the best we can to try to take care of our babies, even as they morph into teenagers and pretend they don't need us. What else could we do to protect them?

Caroline had fallen down the stairs when she was nine months old and ended up with three staples in the top of her sweet, blond, little head. I had been getting the babies out of the bathtub upstairs, and Brian was making me laugh, playing peekaboo with his towel. They had just started to crawl really fast, and the very moment I realized Caroline was no longer in the bathroom with us, I heard the thump, thump, thump of her little body rolling down the stairs. The blood was awful, as is the way with head wounds, but the crying— the crying is something I will remember till I'm an old lady.

We threw Brian into his car seat; I held Caroline in the back seat with a dishcloth on her head; and we made that first ER trip to Portsmouth Hospital. It would not be the last, but the excruciating minutes it took to get there and run her inside were the worst. Then the crying stopped, and she was fixed; she would return to those steps, unafraid of falling again.

14

Allison

We returned to Dr. Lakey's office after school the next day for the results from her four vials of blood. I held Jessie's and Caroline's hands as he diagnosed our daughter with cancer. I could see his mouth moving and watched the words fall from his mustached upper lip, but there was a deafening sound in the room that filled my ears. How could Caroline or Jessie hear any of this? There they sat, listening intently to his words. "Young, healthy, physically fit" rang through, and then Jessie interrupted, her voice breaking my paralysis, "But what will we do next?"

He explained the protocol for a child. She was hardly a child anymore, her rippling triceps now covered in goose bumps as the air-conditioning pumped through the hospital room on a day that had first felt like Indian Summer, one of those last days in fall when the sun heats the earth so much, one feels the urge to argue with Mother Nature that it's not quite time for winter.

We'd only just begun to end our long days. With October only a few weeks away, I was sidetracked momentarily, thinking, "But what about her ski season? Will she be able to race by January?" At that point, I hadn't understood the gravity of all Dr. Lakey was explaining to us. Thankfully, Jessie listened closely, held both our hands tightly, and would be the stabilizing force we all needed if we were to survive the coming months.

Chemotherapy and radiation would be the first lines of defense and, depending on how her body handled those treatments, they would consider a bone marrow transplant. He knew we couldn't handle statistics in that moment, but later I would read online that 70 percent of pediatric cancers can be helped with life-saving bone marrow transplants.

We would all need to be tested to see if any of us could be a match for Caroline's marrow. Dr. Lakey placed high hopes on Brian, her sibling. They had shared so many things up till then—a womb, a room, toys, wagons, birthday parties—of course, it was only natural that his marrow would be a match. This could be taken care of by spring, and she would miss only one season of skiing and maybe have to take it easy in the spring with tennis.

I kept looking over at her, our baby girl. She had aged sitting there in the chair with yellow painted ducks and a child's growth chart on the wall behind her. Jessie and I had been in discussion for weeks that we should probably have her start seeing our doctor instead of the pediatrician. In retrospect, I'm thankful he was the one to give us the news and set up her first appointment in oncology for the very next day.

Caroline allowed us to lead her out to the car as we had so many years earlier, holding her by the hand, tired after tennis lessons or a birthday party or dinner at a friend's house. She didn't say a word the entire drive home from the hospital or even make eye contact in the rearview mirror. Fortunately, during the few miles home, Jessie kept up a steady stream of chatter about the arrangements that would be made and who would make them, prioritizing the important contacts that would need dealing with in the morning.

To keep herself calm, she read the list over several times to make sure we had a proper game plan. In retrospect, I should have let her drive, and I would have sat in the back seat and held Caroline. Brian would be home waiting for us, probably starving after whatever school function he had. My brain was unable to remember if it was drama club or student council, but he would have arrived home on the late bus by four and probably settled in to his homework, knowing that we were with Caroline at the doctor's.

I wanted my mother to hold me. I wanted her to be at the house when we got home. I knew we should be strong for Caroline, but as soon as I closed our bedroom door, I fell apart, knowing that we couldn't keep her safe. How did our parents do this? How did they even send us off to college and not worry about us?

I tried to remember when Mom was the best version of herself. She had been so happy to learn we were pregnant with twins, and our kids have good memories of her skiing with them when they were little. But she started forgetting simple things, and there was the day she kept calling Brian "Joe," which is my brother's name. She kept thinking he was Joe when he was a little boy. At that point, we couldn't leave her alone with the kids, and it was too much for Dad to watch her and the twins. From the day she was diagnosed with Alzheimer's disease to the day she died, only two years passed. She quickly went from being my mother to being a child we all took turns caring for.

Later that night, after everyone was in their rooms, I stood on the deck and whispered into the cold night air, "Mom, I need you to be on your game up there. I know you're organizing some event or bingo game in heaven, so tell all your friends that we need all the prayers we can get right now. I love you, Mom, and miss you every day."

15

Brian

Parents never tell us right away what they ought to tell us. Rather, they try to delay, protect, sugarcoat, what have you. When Moms opened the side door leading from the garage, and Caroline bolted up the stairs to her room without so much as a look at me—not even one begging for sympathy or an intervention, like usual—I thought we were in for a storm.

I had blamed her fatigue and moodiness on hormones. What brother wouldn't? Honestly, living with three women had made me fairly observant of and empathetic to the female plight. Adolescence hadn't been too hard on me. In fact, I think I missed that awkward part of puberty altogether, thank God! Caroline was not holding up as well though, and although we didn't like to admit it, we did love each other, and I would do anything for her—within reason, of course. Like, I wouldn't befriend some guy just to find out if he liked her or anything. That would not be realistic. However, I always try to talk her up at school so that people will give her more of a chance. There are people who would love to be her friend, but they aren't the ones sweating their lives away on the tennis courts or on the slopes.

I poured myself a glass of milk, grabbed a handful of pretzels from the open bag on the counter, and waited for them to tell me how the appointment went, remembering the temper tantrum Caroline had thrown the previous morning about having to leave tennis a few minutes early. I joked about whether Dr. Lakey could fix her being so tense and angry all the time. Both ignored my question, and MJ (Mom Jess when I need to clarify) asked how my school day was, but she didn't really listen to my reply. For kicks, I fabricated a story about Mrs. Whitcher being fired for mentioning that Walt Whitman was gay. No response from either mother. So I tried a different tactic, telling them that the family should consider going vegan as a step in our wellness plan. Again, nothing. I turned to my other mom, held both of her shoulders, and asked in my best fake pilot voice, "Do you read me?"

I was standing there in the kitchen, leaning against the countertop by our new refrigerator the moment she told me about the cancer. I remember the moment like that day in December when those little children and their teachers were killed in Connecticut, the way the generation before mine remembered where they were on September 11, and the generations before that remembered the Challenger disaster and where they were when Kennedy was shot. Caroline's cancer would become our very own Cuban Missile Crisis, a time when we didn't know where to turn, who to tell, and where to take cover.

Mom told me they would need to spend the next few days at the hospital; but they could treat her in Portsmouth, so that was good news. One of them would be home with me at night, and I could not miss school. Unless, of course, there was a day that Caroline really needed me to be there.

The floor suddenly felt cold on my bare feet, and the faucet dripped into the silence, keeping pace with the beating of my heart. They had held it together all day for Caroline's sake, and there in the palpable safety of our warm, citrus kitchen, they collapsed into each other's arms, making it hard to tell where one devastated mother ended and the other began.

I knew Caroline would be okay. I don't know how I knew, but I knew. There were no words to convey that to our mothers though. I stood between them on the outside of their grief ball and wrapped my arms around them both. How small they felt in that instant. I would not cry, not then, because they needed me to be the one to keep it all together. Always good in a crisis, I made a list of the relatives to call, not just because they needed to know, but because Moms needed them to know; they needed all the support they could get.

16

Caroline

I thought it would be easier to have my parents contact my teachers, mostly because I didn't want to see or hear any of those pitiful responses I've seen before when someone's grandmother died or dog had to be put down. Even friends I had in elementary school whose parents got divorced—no one ever really knew what the right thing to say was. I'm sorry your dad left your mom. I'm sorry your mom got fired from her job. I'm sorry your brother got his girlfriend pregnant. I'm sorry you have to move because your house is in foreclosure. I'm sorry your dog died. I'm sorry you have cancer. Then comes the response: Thank you for your sympathy. I probably won't die, at least right away, but again, thank you for your concern. Or I could be flip and funny like Brian. Cancer? What cancer? I have no idea what you're talking about.

No one has written a manual on how to navigate through these kinds of social situations, but I wish someone would. Chapter 10 could be called, "What to Do When a Classmate Develops a Potentially Deadly Disease Like Leukemia?" Followed by chapter 11: "How to Handle Kids Who Hate Your Lesbian Mothers?" Teenagers do not know how to respond to grief well. Even when their intentions are good, they often make a scene, and I knew I could not handle any kind of scene.

Now we're in the process of coming to terms with the fact that we have cancer—we meaning my family, since it is impacting every one of us a little differently. I have an oncology team who will draw up a battle strategy for me. They will decide how much chemotherapy and how often; determine whether radiation is another option; and, lastly, create my list of potential blood marrow donors.

I like being goal oriented. Treating this disease is going to be like an athletic competition. As long as I stay focused, determined, and physically strong, I'm unbeatable. However, I'm worried about Moms and how they're going to hold up under the stress. My pain threshold is high, so while I have no idea the pain associated with the chemicals they will put into my body, I'm optimistic that I can handle it.

Parents just can't handle watching their kids suffer, which is why I haven't told them the half of what's been happening at school these last two years, with that group of girls acting anywhere between five and twenty-five in any given moment. I've just decided there are mean girls everywhere, and I've handled difficult situations well enough that they know they aren't getting to me, because I'm not a weak person. I'm a strong person. If those girls think I'm going to die, even if I'm not, maybe they will think twice about treating others like they belong on the bottom of their shoes.

Brian told me he would take care of things at school, like collecting my books and getting my assignments from teachers; he also told me I couldn't die, because he couldn't handle the moms by himself. That last part did get a smile out of me. It cracks me up when he refers to them as the moms, as if they are a force of nature, which they are. He is a good brother.

It would probably be better if both moms drove home at night to be with him, just for some normalcy, but I might get lonely there all by myself, at least that first night. Dr. Lakey and the new oncologist, Dr. O'Hara, feel optimistic that a donor will be easy to find, but we will need to start that soon. First though, they have to kill the bad cells in my marrow to make room for the good ones, which should take over and start producing healthy blood cells. Only then will I be in remission.

This is going to sound strange, but I know I'm going to be okay. Don't ask me how I know, because there is nothing rational about it, other than this weird sixth sense about my life not ending this way. Hearing the news I have cancer was awful, especially because I've never been sick, despite being born teeny tiny and at risk and having neurotic mothers hovering over my entire childhood. People have told me over the years that I have an old soul, so maybe the person I was in another life was destined to be me in this one, which gives me this internal courage I can feel radiate from my bones. Maybe even directly from my marrow.

Marrow is the spot in bones where the production of red and white blood cells takes place. I'm sure it was Henry David Thoreau who talked about "living deeply and sucking the marrow from life." He went on to talk about how he did not "want to learn when it came time to die that he had not lived." He was a profound guy. I'm going to think about my marrow and the possibility of having to use someone's marrow to kick this disease out of my body. Our moms are already getting jazzed up to organize a drive to find someone to match me. They're going to contact the biological owners of our genes to see if they and their children can be tested. Weird, right?

Just thinking about the potential that Brian and I have other siblings in the world takes my mind off the possibility that I could die from this disease. Or maybe it's just the shock of being fourteen years old, on the cusp of everything I've ever felt possible in life, and knowing that God couldn't possibly strip that from me now. Or thinking of Moms, two people who loved each other so completely that they felt compelled to adopt us in our embryonic states just for the chance at loving a child of their own. I know horrible things happen to good people every day, but this is not one of those days, and I'm not one of those people.

17

Andrew

Moritomo's in Concord has some of the best sushi north of Boston. Honestly, I've traveled this world quite a bit, and one would not think a little city like Concord, New Hampshire, could boast such quality. Elizabeth and I met for dinner here frequently before we had kids. If we were shopping SoCo (south of Concord), this was the natural spot for us to stop on our way home.

I was really looking forward to our problem-solving session tonight over a spicy tuna roll. One, because I knew we had a lot to talk about, and, two, being out of town allows us both to let our guard down. We weren't likely to run into anyone we knew, so even if the place was packed, we could be guaranteed the intimacy that parents of teenagers don't get often enough.

As much as I knew I would enjoy the meal and the company, and I love Elizabeth with all my being, even more than I did when we married, the conversation was going to be hard. What were we going to do with Michelle? That's about all I thought we would talk about. Nothing could have prepared me for the news that Elizabeth shared with me as she sat across the table and sipped her diet Coke with lemon.

I was right about her having a plan for Stephen, although I had no idea his grades were dropping. It took all of my mental fortitude not to order myself a gin and tonic, because I knew how important it was to her that I appear in control on the outside, even if I was a chaotic mess on the inside. She had made a list, of course; lists ruled her world, and in this instance, I was grateful. Incredibly grateful. She told me what was going to happen. On Monday, we had an appointment with Stephen's guidance counselors and team of teachers.

My first thought was to reject this; he was a junior, so what business did we have busting into that school to talk grades? Back in my day, I either did the work or I didn't. My parents accepted whatever grades I earned, knowing I would be the one to face the consequences. However, when it came to most matters of education, I deferred to Elizabeth, as she was the professor in the family.

Then she talked about how much his counselor was worried about him being more withdrawn than usual, and I realized I couldn't remember the last time he and I had just laughed together over something stupid on television or gone and done something together. He had lost interest in skiing with us around middle school, when all he wanted to do was play his music on the weekends. We didn't want to push him to ski if he was miserable doing it. My hope was that one day he would find himself missing it, but maybe that was it—maybe we should have kept him doing something active or outdoors so he didn't spend so much time cooped up in his room.

Next on Elizabeth's list was a meeting at Michelle's soccer coach's house for dessert Tuesday night. Elizabeth had called Dena, a friend for years who also happened to be Michelle's varsity coach since eighth grade. Michelle had babysat her children over the years, which had been the best birth control a mentor could impose upon a teenager. The expectation was that Michelle would explain the drunken incident to her and discuss consequences.

Soccer season was in full swing, and Michelle hadn't been arrested, fortunately. But she had broken the school's athletic code, in which she'd promised not to drink or use drugs or behave in any way that was unbefitting for a teenage role model. Furthermore, she had broken the law, and Elizabeth understood even better than I did that Dena would give Michelle the kind of "I'm disappointed in you" talk that would make her listen far better than she would to either one of us.

I agreed it was important for both of us to be there to support Michelle. Michelle's always been such an amazing kid, and I realized that even the best of kids make mistakes. God knows we did. However, decisions like the ones Michelle made can have nasty consequences. And, while my life in a wheelchair has been fulfilling in many ways, I still think about the night of my accident, of everything that led up to it, and of every consequence that followed. I wanted her to understand that it could have been so much worse; she could have died from alcohol poisoning or been humiliated with photos on social media. What if she had been raped? Or had fallen down, hit her head on a rock, and lost her ability to think, speak, or walk? Or worse?

The last thing on Elizabeth's list was the most memorable. We were drinking green tea at that point, and she set her cup down and held my hand across the table, something she had not done in years, I think. She told me to take three deep breaths. Good god, woman! How bad could it be? Did she have breast cancer? Did she want a divorce? Did I screw up our taxes so badly the IRS wanted to investigate my business? The next words to escape her lips left me floating over our table, looking down at us sitting there, a couple in love, holding hands across the table, with a daughter who would hate us for holding her accountable for her actions, her one big mistake so far, and a son who has been sad, but no one has noticed until now, and then this? and a son who had been sad, but no one has noticed until now, and then this?

64

18

Elizabeth

I held his hands and looked into his face, a face still so handsome after all of these years. I cleared my throat and took three deep breaths to match his. "There are twins who were born from our embryos almost fifteen years ago." Before he had a chance to reply or ask a question, I added the fact that one of them, a girl named Caroline, needed our help—that we could help her. She had been in and out of the hospital for the last few months, battling pediatric acute leukemia, and she needed a bone marrow transplant.

He was silent.

"Andrew, please say something."

He just looked at me as if the air in his lungs had been vacuumed out. So I kept talking, hoping he would relax his painfully tight hold on my hands. "All those years ago," I reminded him, "we had checked off the box that we could be contacted through the courts on the occasion the adoptive family needed to learn our identities."

The phrase "adoptive family" was the one I had been most afraid to utter again. That had been almost sixteen years ago, and I had begun to think that his feelings had changed.

His voice crackled to interrupt my ramble only to ask what I knew about them. I pretended that he meant the children and could only say what had been told to me on the phone, which was not very much. It was not the time to tell him about Stephen impersonating him on the phone with the social worker.

I'd had an evening class last week, the same day Stephen decided to take it upon himself to call Casey Chase and ask for more information. When I returned home, Michelle, who was still on lockdown, as she called her punishment, had already gone to bed, and Stephen sat at the kitchen table with the piece of paper and envelope in front of him. He handed me the letter and told me it was probably something I should read, since it involved his biological brother or sister.

"Stephen, let me explain," I had pleaded with him.

"Why don't you just read the letter first?" he suggested in a demanding, almost parental, tone. I placed my hand on the pine kitchen table, stained over the years by various craft projects, pots that were too hot, scratches from Matchbox cars, and nicks from knives when someone didn't want to take the time to use a cutting board.

I had known. I had known all along that other babies had been born. I had known and not told Andrew, not because I wanted to keep it a secret from him, but because he hadn't seemed to need to know like I did. I had known and not told him. Now I would need to tell him and explain to our almost adult children about their unknown genetic relations.

Using the table to steady my balance, I read the letter, which asked us to call Casey Chase, the social worker at Dartmouth, regarding an anonymity clause. This paperwork requested that we allow the adoptive family to contact us directly due to a medical emergency. Stephen handed me a faxed copy of what appeared to be a permission form. The look on my face compelled him to respond, "I figured you and Dad would want to help, so I just had him fax the form to me at school."

Just like that, Stephen had known the right thing to do; we would help out, of course. They could contact us directly, and we would do whatever we needed to. Only I wished I had told Andrew this already.

"Thank you, honey," was about all I could muster in that moment, but I knew Stephen deserved more of an explanation. "Can we talk about this more when your sister is here, so I only need to explain it once?" I stood there in my raincoat, school bag dropped at my feet, waiting for a response. The look on his face was similar to what Andrew's would be when I told him. Not anger. Not betrayal. Not happiness. Not shock. Rather, sheer confusion.

"Sure, we can wait for Michelle, and we probably ought to clue Dad in too, right? Don't worry, Mom, I did the right thing."

"What do you mean? What did you do exactly?" My heart pounded in my chest.

"I gave them verbal permission to give our name and address to the family so that they could contact us directly to inquire about whether we would be tested. I'm assuming the right thing is for us all to be tested. Right? Right, Mom? Mom, what's wrong with you?"

What had possessed him, I wondered, the young man who had hardly said three words lately, to decide to call a social worker's office and pretend to be his father? Dear God. I needed to make a list. So I made the list, one of many I make on a daily basis, sometimes on paper, sometimes on the notes app on my phone, and sometimes on random objects like cardboard boxes or paper bags, if that's all I have at hand. And so I was thankful to have my list that night with Andrew at Moritomo's when I dropped the bomb on his lap. The list had six things on it:

1. Tell Andrew about the twins.

2. Tell Andrew about Stephen's appointment in guidance.

3. Tell Andrew about meeting at Dena's house.

4. Tell Andrew I love him.

5. Tell Andrew about Stephen impersonating him on the phone.

6. Tell Andrew we will get through this.

When Andrew did not respond— could not respond—I almost expected him to storm out of the restaurant. I looked back down at the list handwritten on a yellow sticky note, and numbers four and six triggered me to remind him how much I loved him and that this would not be the worst thing in the world to happen to us. "I love you, Andrew, and our children need us, the ones we are raising, and the ones we simply helped to create."

"I need time to process this and will see you at home, Elizabeth," he said. "Please drive carefully." Those were his last words to me in that conversation.

19

Michelle

I'm asleep. Or at least I think I must be sleeping, because what I'm feeling must certainly be a dream. This girl. She visits me sometimes in my sleep. It's not one of those repetitive dreams I had as a kid, where a dinosaur is chasing me, or I'm lost in the grocery store and can't find Mom. Rather, it's the kind of dream I have when it feels like I'm hovering above my own life, floating above myself, looking down on and wondering where I am.

The girl is about my age, wears her hair short and brown, and sits on the swing of the playground of my elementary school. She watches me, and I know I'm dreaming because as soon as I try to approach her, she disappears. Not like *poof* gone, but more like a slow, foggy dissipation, so that by the time I'm standing next to the swing, I'm almost not sure exactly that she was ever swinging there in the first place.

When I first started dreaming about her, I asked my psych teacher what it could mean, and she referred me to one of her books on dream interpretation. Sometimes, according to the dream expert whose name I can't remember, when we are stressed, our minds try to use other problem-solving strategies. Maybe this girl—teenager really—was trying to help me to figure out my stress. Today, she has on red cowboy boots, jeans, a wool sweater, and a homemade knit hat; she waves to me, smiling.

Clearly, she is not someone to be afraid of. Would I be friends with her at school? Maybe. Although, the cowboy boots are red, she strikes me as a quiet person, but maybe she is one of those quiet on the inside, loud on the outside kinds of kids. My mother would say she is an old soul, that she has the look and feel of someone who has lived a long time, even though in a kid's body. Or maybe hers is a soul that has lived before. Maybe she is a spirit who has to help a certain number of people before she can get all the way to heaven. Maybe she has already been to heaven, and she visits people in their dreams who need help. Damn, could I use some help.

My afternoon nap in lockdown ended quickly when I hear my parents barking at each other in the kitchen downstairs. I've given them a lot to argue about lately. So has Stephen. Mostly, I've humiliated them. What they don't understand is how much I've embarrassed myself. "Look," I tried explaining to them at one point, "even the best of kids make mistakes!"

"But yours," Dad countered, "may have cost you everything you've worked so hard to achieve as a senior."

This whole lockdown thing, I would like to argue, is ridiculous. Just because I screwed up one time. Well, maybe this was the one time I was caught, and that's why I feel so awful about it.

We met with Coach after school yesterday, before the practice that would be happening without me. I hated to let anyone down, especially her. I just didn't think it through when Courtney and I decided to drink out in the woods that night. I figured we would drink a bit with everyone in the woods and then I would just sleep over with no worries. No harm done. Then I had to overdo it, pass out, and make her think I was dead from alcohol poisoning. That's where it all started to go bad.

Now, Mom, who believes in this tough love thing—even though I wasn't arrested, nor did I destroy property, sleep with a boy, do drugs, operate a vehicle under the influence, or hurt someone's feelings—made me tell Coach what I had done. Coach agreed with her that I should step off the team according to the athletics policy. She was required to tell the administration, and she wasn't going to play me any more either; I hadn't been fair to my team.

She told me this story about a girl who graduated five or six years ago who came to her to admit to smoking pot on Labor Day weekend. The girl drove to her house to tell Coach, because she didn't feel right keeping it from her. She knew the consequence was being kicked off the team for thirty school days, which was her whole season. No one turned her in; she just didn't want to live with the guilt. Coach told this girl, also a senior at the time, that she was so proud of her for telling the truth, especially when the girl's mother didn't even want her to tell. Her team was let down, for sure, but the girl was able to maintain integrity in the end.

This story was meant to help me see the "bigger picture," but I can't stand when adults do that. The damn bigger picture doesn't mean shit to me right now.

However, since it was my first "offense" and there was no arrest or need to go to court, Coach could help me to maintain my reputation at school. This way, my letters of recommendations to colleges, which had already been written and submitted in some cases, would remain unblemished.

She also wanted me to apologize to my teammates, which was probably the worst peer experience I've ever had. The part that killed me the most was that Courtney was still on the team. Her parents wouldn't do what mine did. They kept "the blue tarp incident" to themselves, probably because they didn't want anyone to think their parenting skills were less than perfect.

I vaguely remembered the girl from my dreams coming to see me as Courtney's dad dragged me out of the woods on the tarp. Of course, none of this made sense in that moment, but she was trying to tell me that someone needed my help. I remember thinking, *Does she need my help instead of me needing hers?*

But it wasn't worth reliving over and over again, so I opened my bedroom door to the world, deciding prisoners are fed dinner, even in lockdown. The house was quiet. I couldn't even hear Stephen playing his music in his room. Maybe he needed my help. He needed something all right; that kid was not right in the head. But I'd been so caught up in my shit, I paid him no attention. Come to think of it, I hadn't even seen him sit with his few band friends at lunch the last few weeks. Where had he been eating lunch? And my parents think that I'm the big problem right now. Ridiculous.

As I walked down the creaky wooden stairs, I saw the light from my dad's office through the bottom of the door. Fight over. Both sides had retreated into their corners, apparently to rest for following rounds.

Stephen was sitting at the kitchen table while Mom shuttled plates of food from the stove. "Michelle, please tell Dad dinner is ready, and we would like to eat as a family since we are all home." Ugh, the whole eating as a family thing was overrated on days where clearly no one needed or wanted to say anything kind to each other.

Stephen looked up at me, his eyes big with worry. The family was falling apart. I was falling apart. Stephen is a stress ball, and my parents, although far from perfect, had always done a good job of keeping their own conflicts relatively private. I never thought they were unhappy together until now. I am never having children. Seriously, we used to look like we had it together, and, now, when I know so many other families have it worse, I'm embarrassed we aren't handling our own stress very gracefully. I hated knocking on his door. When I was younger, we just burst in, no knocking and no privacy. As soon as I started wanting them to grant me privacy, I suddenly started giving them theirs, which resulted in many closed doors in a house that was meant to be open.

20

Stephen

Mom wanted me to explain to Dad about my impersonation of him on the phone. This was going to be our family dinner conversation—discussion, argument, blowup. Whatever it was, it would be ugly; I could feel it in my soul.

Dad cleared his throat, and I knew it was coming. But first, as he passed me the broccoli, he casually inquired, "How are things going in band, son?" This threw me off, as I was unprepared for this line of questioning; not that he was interrogating me or anything, but I had been ready to answer to "Son, why did you call the social worker and pretend to be me?" Shit, they had to have finally looked at my progress reports. Kinda late at that point, since another three weeks had passed, and quarter grades were closing rapidly.

I placed some broccoli mindlessly on my plate and passed it along to my sister, who gave me the hairy eyeball, as if to say, "Speak up, and take a little pressure off of me for once!"

"Band is fine, really fine. I struggled a little at the beginning of the year, but it's coming together okay now." I knew exactly why he had asked and wondered what their game plan was, since they had been harsh with laying the smackdown on Michelle, forcing her to step off the team. I could only imagine what they had in store for me. In retrospect, I realized a failing grade in band is a total red flag of something being really wrong with me, since band had always been my favorite class. My teacher is awesome too; he is really funny, sarcastic, loves to challenge us. But lately I haven't been liking the music we're playing in band and would rather just write and play my own at home.

Again, Dad cleared his throat. "Well, your mother and I are meeting with your guidance counselor, Ms. Hollos, and the band director, Mr. Clermont, tomorrow before school, and we expect you to come with us to the meeting." He continued to cut his chicken and scrape his fork across the plate, unaware that noise makes me *want to scream*. I was suddenly sidetracked by the scraping, wondering how some people are not aware of the noises they make while eating.

Michelle kicked me under the table, and I was brought back to the conversation. I decided that if I ate, I couldn't talk. I picked up my fork to take a bite of my rice pilaf and suddenly was not hungry at all. If I stopped eating altogether, my mother would be completely baffled by her younger child, and I certainly didn't want to cause her any more stress.

After asking to be excused, Michelle took her plate to the sink, turned to our parents, and came right out with questions I was thinking would be the focus of our dinner. "What is up with the kid with cancer who needs our bone marrow? How is she related to us? How do we get tested? Do we get to meet them? Where do they live? How old are they?" Apparently, all this time on lockdown had her thinking about something else.

As I'd had the initial conversation with Casey Chase, I felt compelled to speak first. "Well, Michelle, apparently, we aren't the only ones in this family keeping secrets from one another. About sixteen years ago, Mom and Dad made it possible for another couple to have a family by putting their leftover embryos up for adoption.

So, there is this girl who has leukemia, and she is our biological sister, right, Mom? And her parents are lesbians, right, Mom?"

Silence. Dad dropped his fork and knife. The clatter startled us all. The secondary letter had arrived with the return address reading, "Allison and Jessica Lakewood." Call me crazy, but neither of those names could be masculine. Judging by Mom's face, she hadn't shown Dad the follow-up letter after the anonymity clause had been lifted. Oops. But really, I wasn't sorry. This was the most alive our family had felt in a long time, and the pressure was off me.

Mom's face showed the composure she must have learned in the classroom when her students were disrespectful or aloof or hung over and acting like idiots. I couldn't even look at my father. However, I was on a roll at that point, and I knew we would all be tested to see if we were a genetic match for this girl.

My parents are good people, and they would want to do the right thing, but I was angry. How could they not have told us this? How could they have kept from us the fact that we had other siblings out there? What "right time" could they possibly be waiting for? I wanted to hurt them for not paying better attention, for the fact that hardly anyone noticed that I hadn't been coming out of my room for a year except to eat meals. Yet there is this girl we've never met—a sibling who needed our help or she might die. And tomorrow I have to sit in a room with them and listen to Ms. Hollos say to me, like we've practiced, "Stephen, is there anything you want to say to your parents about why school has been harder for you this year?"

In that moment, I'm just supposed to turn to them and say, "Because I think I might be gay, and my father is homophobic, and it scares me that he isn't going to love me anymore." Because if she thinks I'm going to be able to say all that tomorrow morning before school, she has another thing coming. The reason my grades are so bad in band is because Mr. Clermont was the first person I felt comfortable talking to about it, and he concluded that I might be depressed or that maybe someone in guidance should know. I guess I wanted them to know, or I wouldn't have said anything to Mr. Clermont. I'm just so distracted from thinking so hard about everything that I can't focus on even the good stuff, like my music.

Teachers and parents always try to make you feel bad by saying life could be so much worse if, say, we lived in Afghanistan or even in a really poor neighborhood, where the school couldn't afford good books for its students. I should be thankful and appreciate what I have. This girl has cancer, and she might die. I might be gay. I'm not sure. I stopped doing my work. I don't like to leave my bedroom. A teacher worried and asked me if I was okay. I was honest and said no. Look where that has gotten me.

21

Jessie

We knew the likelihood of us being a good donor match was slim, but neither of us could sit around waiting for a match to be found and not do anything. So, as soon as Caroline finished her first round of chemotherapy, we threw ourselves into establishing blood marrow drives; the first being at her school, because students could be tested at age sixteen with parental consent. No luck. There was another one at Portsmouth Hospital and another near Allison's vet clinic. No luck still.

In the meantime, we had contacted Dartmouth about releasing the anonymity clause on our embryo donors' identity. The donors agreed to lift the anonymity clause, but they were taking their sweet time in contacting us or being tested. Their names are Andrew and Elizabeth Walker, and we sent them a letter. This could be our only viable hope long-term, Caroline's best chance at survival. These people obviously had at least one child, so that could be up to three people who could match her marrow.

We had to sit down and talk with Brian and Caroline about the fact that they may be meeting their biological parents in the near future, unless those parents decided they didn't want to be contacted. Or, God forbid, something devastating happened to their child or to their family, and they are no longer living.

What could possibly be taking that family's so long to respond? This should be instant; we should have received notice the following day. Why would parents say no to being tested? Would they allow their child or children to be tested? Do their children know the situation? Ours have known all along, clearly, that they were not ours biologically, and, for Brian, that has never been an issues. But with Caroline, always an issue. She doesn't want to meet them. She would just like to get their marrow and be done with it.

And the poor kid, she has been through a lot these last months. Her body is no longer hers to do with what she chooses, and she is at that age where kids are so self-conscious about their bodies. She has always been a competitor, and the fact that her physical attributes are failing her now is an abomination, and the chemo has worn her down. She has lost her beautiful, thick hair, and although she has enough fun wigs to wear, she prefers her favorite winter hat, the blue one with a green pom-pom her grandmother knit years ago, which she wears to the mountain on weekends. Her skin is paper thin, dry, and crackly, and she has no immune system to speak of.

But one good thing that has happened; a few of her friends from elementary school have resurfaced and come by the house a few times to say hello, bringing her news from school. Of course, Caroline believes that this is just a sympathy visitation: no one wanted to be her friend when she was kicking everyone's ass on the tennis court or race course, but now that she might die, nobody wants to be accused of being unfriendly.

Brian has been steadfast with his sister. He's the only one who can make her laugh on a regular basis. When the last of her hair fell out a few weeks ago, he made a point to take a trip to the barber for a matching haircut. Since that day, a few of his classmates have followed suit, claiming the trendiness of a bald head. Brian just laughs and says it's much easier to take care of; no longer does he have to worry about the lice dilemma in the schools or the peer pressure of whether to gel or not to gel, spike up in front or leave parted to one side. No one can tell if he hasn't showered in days, and the fact that he is six feet tall with no facial hair also makes him a bit of an anomaly.

He continues to raise himself independently and doesn't complain if he has to eat a tuna sandwich for dinner because we were all at the hospital or if it's pizza for the third night in one week. He even bought toilet paper the other day because we had run out.

I should probably place a call to their guidance counselor, Ms. Bartlett, just to make sure he's handling himself there as well as he appears to be here at home. Clearly, our focus has been on Caroline, and she needs us more right now. However, I certainly don't want Brian to feel abandoned. He does have a tight-knit group of friends whose parents have taken on the load of helping him get to the many activities he's involved in.

Polly and Tony Cunningham have been unbelievable neighbors, picking Brian up, walking the dogs when needed, making meals on occasion, and just overall taking care of our family. They are the best kind of people, showing their support when it's needed or even when it isn't. On more than one occasion, I've stopped by their house after a rough day, and Polly has given me one of her fantastic hugs and told me I'm a wonderful mother and Caroline will be okay.

These two have been the best surrogates for my own parents. Tony has shoveled a path around the house and snowplowed the driveway for us after each storm, just to make sure we had multiple exits in case of an emergency. They even attended Brian's art show and holiday concert so someone from "the family" was there. It happened to be on a night when Ally had an emergency surgery at her hospital, and Caroline was having a hard time adjusting to a new round of chemotherapy. Brian played off our not being there, saying, "Don't worry, there will plenty of opportunities to support me in my future life of fame and glory. Tony and Polly were there to cheer me on tonight and even treated me to hot cocoa afterward."

My work as a graphic designer has allowed me to take considerable time off, and current clients are understanding. Thank God for their flexibility. Donna has picked up much of my slack, and Ruthie keeps the office running on a daily basis. I'm terrible at the creative aspect of my work anyway, since I can't focus on anything but Caroline's health and constant communication with the hospital. Allison has cut way back on her time at work, but she still needs to go to the office every day, unless Caroline has a procedure, chemo, or consult.

The good news is that we have another marrow drive coming up on Friday, and any of these people could have the power to save Caroline's life. I hate to put so much emphasis on the results of the embryo donor reveal, but I feel like this is our best shot at beating Caroline's cancer.

22

Allison

Brian was helping me to make dinner while Caroline and Jessie had gone to look for a birthday present for Brian. Their fifteenth birthdays are rapidly approaching, and Caroline really needs to get out of the house. Her tutoring sessions at home aren't keeping her focused on the work that still needs to be done. She doesn't want to be behind her class, but she also can't attend school until her immune system is better.

Casey Chase, the social worker from the hospital, called to say they finally had consent from one of the biological parents and one of the children, who is eighteen. They need consent from both parents to test the younger of the children. Why in God's name would one parent not provide consent in a situation like this? It's not like they don't believe in intervening with natural processes; they conceived a child at a fertility clinic! If the roles were reversed, I bet their ass they would want the parents to sign the consent form. If only we could meet them in person, we could make them understand. If only we could bring them to our home and show them the love that this family thrives on.

I was cutting vegetables for the salad rather emphatically and felt Brian's hand on my arm. Gently, he said to me, "Do you think the adult in that family who hasn't given consent is uncomfortable with our family?" Then in a whisper, "Do you think he or she is unsupportive of the fact that two women are raising their offspring?"

That Brian was even suggesting this to me broke his heart, because this was the last thing he wanted to remind me of—besides the fact that we could lose Caroline because the one person who could save her was afraid of us. The insanity.

I started to remind Brian of what regular people we are—"We are just a family who loves each other!"—and suddenly I was crying into the sweatshirt on Brian's man-sized shoulders. He held me close and repeated softly, "I know. I know. I know," as I break down and sob like the baby I've always been when it comes to the health of our children.

23

Brian

"But, Mom," I said, "the good news is that at least one of the parents is willing to be tested, and we know their names. Then we'll know the identity of the asshole who refuses to help us. We can put on black ninja outfits, borrow a shady van, kidnap the guy, and beat him into submission like they do on the movies." There it was—a smile.

Violence would not fly with Moms or even with me, really. I was that kid who caught spiders and let them go outside. I was trying to build some hope back into her. The fact that these people were my actual genetic relations hadn't really settled in yet; until this point, these efforts had all been in the hope of getting Caroline some help fast.

"Remember, Brian, just because one of them agreed to be tested doesn't mean they want to know anything about us. Please don't get your hopes up." Her eyes darted to the sound of the garage door opening. Mom had returned from the mall with Caroline.

"So we write another letter, this one from me, and ask that it be delivered to them ASAP. We can pay extra for that, right? Overnight it to them? Mom, you know how convincing I am with my words. Just let them try to deny me my sister's health!" The door to the garage opened, and in they came. Caroline was smiling, a little happier, having been out of the house for a while.

"That bag isn't big enough to hold my birthday present," I teased.

"Don't be a jerk," she said with a laugh, hitting me with it as she walked by.

Using my best sarcasm, I continued, "I just don't want you to feel all important all the time, Sis. The world revolves around Caroline, blah, blah, blah, just because she has cancer, blah, blah, blah! I'm the one holding this family together, for the love of Pete! Look at you people; you're a mess! Mom, I get that you wear sweatpants in the comfort of your own home, but to the mall? Really? And you, Mom, when was the last time you washed those jeans you've been in for a week straight? At least Caroline pulls herself together with a fun hat or scarf. You two probably didn't brush your teeth today. Well, it's a good thing I can make a mean salad to accompany Mom's veggie chili, or we wouldn't have a damn thing to eat. If no one is offended yet, I'm going to take a bowl of this to my room, as I have a writing project to work on for school."

"Oh, really, is it something I'm supposed to work on, too?" Caroline asked. "You know I don't want to get more behind than I already am."

I couldn't help myself. "You should do a fake assignment as well, if you're feeling up to it. I wasn't going to put the assignment on you tonight, since you're surely exhausted from all the shopping for my birthday present. Anyway, we're supposed to write a descriptive essay about a sibling relationship we have either with our actual sibling or a friend who is as close to you as a sibling. No hard feelings if you don't want to write about me, but I'm going to write about you. Think about it as my birthday gift to you."

"Very funny. How long does it have to be? Typed, double-spaced? Was there a handout?"

I rolled my eyes and thanked teachers silently again for their unbelievable patience with kids like her. Then I made up some fake stats for the fake assignment and retired to my room.

Sitting at my desk, I tried to think of the best way to begin a letter to the other family. Would it be better to write to the eighteen-year-old? The mother? The father? The kid not old enough to be tested? Maybe a letter to each of them. That would take forever.

Well, let's start with one, the problem adult, guessing it is the dad. To Whom It May Concern …

24

Caroline

When I'm home doing normal teenage kid stuff like sitting down to dinner with Moms or shopping at the mall or fighting with Brian over what to watch on the one TV we have—though everyone else we know seems to have a TV or computer in every room of the house— or putting my laundry away or pulling out the wad of long hair in my tub drain and Brian freaking out on me, I don't really think about having cancer or dying.

But when I'm sitting in the hospital, or driving to or from the hospital, or scheduling another round of something, or following up with the marrow drive results, or reading emails from my teachers about completing my work "only when feeling up to it" and not worrying because there will be plenty of time to catch up when I'm all better—only then do I really think about dying.

I wonder how much worse I'm going to feel before I get better. I don't really question the "if" I get better. I do the positive visualization that the family therapist from the hospital taught me how to do. She used to be a health and PE teacher, and then she went back to school so she could work with kids in crisis, like me.

I drink my fluids and handle my chemo like a champ. Another round coming up next week. But this has been a good week. And next week will be a shitty week, and I'll throw up everything I try to eat, and my head will pulse all day every day, and my mouth will be filled with sores and on fire, and my scalp will itch, and I will scratch it with my fingernails that don't grow anymore, and the nurses and doctors and Moms will say, "Is there anything I can get you to make this easier?" and my only reply will be, "Yes, some good and healthy marrow to fill my bones with."

I turn my head back to whatever book I'm reading. They've filled my room at home with autobiographies and biographies of powerful women, professional athletes, and good fiction for when I need to take a break from thinking so hard. I know how hard Moms have been working to make me as comfortable as possible, whether I'm at home or at the hospital. I also know whatever time they aren't with me or working at their jobs, they're working around the clock to see that all of their friends and friends of friends and friends of friends of friends have had their bone marrow tested. And maybe the family we have yet to meet?

So then there is that too. If I hadn't been sick, would I have ever learned the identity of the people who put my former embryonic state up for adoption? Do I want to know them? Or is having their marrow enough? I wonder what Brian thinks about all of this—Mr. I Never Take Anything Seriously. I know he worries about me too. He's been solid through this whole ordeal, never complaining, except to make us laugh.

Last night, I left my bedroom and saw his bedroom door closed, but the light was still coming from underneath. "Brian." I knocked gently in case he had fallen asleep. No response. I turned the doorknob, knowing it wouldn't be locked, because he kept nothing from the world. Sure enough, he was lying on his side, fetal position style, papers and laptop spread around the lower half of his body.

The Spiderman alarm clock, the one he's had since the Christmas when we were six, read 9:07, and I was relieved that the boy does sleep at some point. The same Christmas, I had asked Santa for an alarm clock too, but I wanted an old-fashioned one with hands on it like my grandmother had by her bedside. Not that I could even tell time at that point, but it was important to me not to be treated like a baby.

Sleep doesn't come easily to me anymore; therefore, I envy most people who do it so naturally.

I picked up Brian's papers to drape a blanket over his body. For being six feet, he still looks like a baby in many ways—no stubble to speak of, and his sheets still sport Curious George, making me smile. His room is the eclectic combo of theater posters and artwork; he's really gotten good at the whole stage acting gig. As I stacked the papers on his desk, "To Whom It May Concern" caught my eye.

If you are reading this letter, you are either my biological mother or father, and my name is Brian. I am fourteen years old, a straight-A student involved in drama and the arts at Portsmouth High School. My twin sister is Caroline, and she has leukemia. I've been thinking about the reason you haven't signed over consent for your youngest child to be tested for his/her bone marrow. Or why you yourself haven't agreed to be tested. Are you afraid of knowing us? Is it because perhaps you are uncomfortable having learned our mothers are lesbians?

That being said, you would not feel uncomfortable around Caroline in the least. She is the smartest, most competitive athlete in our school.

Seriously, she could play Division I tennis or ski race at the professional level, which is not bad for a girl who lives near the ocean. The thing is, she must get that from someone in your family, because it certainly doesn't come from ours. Don't get me wrong; I'm well-rounded, liked by my peers, and great with the ladies at school, if I do say so myself; I love performing on stage and speaking in public. Some of those natural abilities also do not come from being raised by our mothers, who, by the way, are the most doting and nurturing women on the planet—to a fault almost. They can be intensely overprotective. For example, I couldn't go into the men's room *anywhere* till I was almost freakin' eleven years old. That just about killed me. They love us to a point of smothering and then some.

We were really sick because we were born early, but you would never know it now to look at us— well, to look at me anyway. Six foot even, 170 pounds of burning love is how I like to describe myself, with brown hair and brown eyes. But if you want to see something truly beautiful, you should see my sister when she isn't sick. Even now that she is sick, her eyes are so crazy intense that it feels they are reading your very soul. Don't ever tell her I'm telling you this because, as a brother, it's my job to keep her guessing. I'm enclosing a picture of her so that you can picture saying no directly to her in person as opposed to through an anonymous mail carrier or social worker, which would be far easier.

Caroline deserves this chance at life. She works harder to be better than everyone at everything. Personally, this makes her slightly socially awkward because she doesn't have a ton of friends. However, girls seem to be weirder anyway in adolescence; not sure what experience you have there at your house, but living with three women is *not* easy. So, I'm inclined to believe that one of you in that household is going to be the person—well, your marrow, actually, is going to be what saves the day, or saves my sister's life.

I have to believe that you are a good person, because if you didn't care about the potential for life, you would have just discarded those leftover embryos all those years ago. But you didn't. You put them up for adoption. And I'm also guessing that you must have wanted to be parents desperately to go through fertility treatments.

So here I am. And here is my sister, Caroline, and while our blood, bones, and all the other genetic stuff come from you guys, our moms gave us life and have given us everything we have ever needed since the day we were born. Unfortunately, they cannot give Caroline what she needs most right now, and neither can I. Please help. You are our only hope. Thank you for understanding,

Brian
P.S. If you feel like calling directly, I can be reached on my cell, 603-254-4772, or at home, 603-424-9861.

This was the first thing that made me cry since being told I had leukemia. I put his papers on his desk, made sure the blankets were pulled around him, shut off his light, and walked down the hall to my room, quietly weeping.

25

Andrew

I didn't sign the consent form for Stephen, nor did I want to be tested myself, nor did I want this family to know my identity, but clearly it was too late for that. Elizabeth had kept something this important to herself all of those years, and I'm not sure how to forgive her for that. She claims I couldn't handle the knowledge. She doesn't give me enough credit. Plus, she made me feel stupid in front of our children.

I remember her saying something about how I would feel if someone treated me unkindly or differently due to my injury or being in a wheelchair, making a comparison to being uncomfortable around gay people. She doesn't know why this is such a complicated subject for me. I suppose I should have told her years ago, but it's not as simple a situation as she views it. I can't go back and change what I did in the past.

So I didn't respond because I thought she was asking rhetorically, but maybe that was her way of "feeling me out" regarding the knowledge she had about the family who adopted our embryos. So, when the first letter came, the one Stephen intercepted, I responded as any father would who had begun to feel the seams of his family unraveling: I said no abruptly, stubbornly, and without exception.

And yet, now, as I sit here alone in our bedroom, while Elizabeth is on the phone with her sister, Mimi, I know exactly what is happening in our family. We stopped paying attention. We took for granted that our amazing children would always make the right choices. They are hard workers, have a good combination of both my and Elizabeth's personalities, and seem to have made the right kinds of friendships at school. But with all of this trouble the two of them are having, I feel as if I'm back to learning how to use my wheelchair again, back to all of that bullshit in rehab that I hated. I had to dress myself and make a meal and wonder incessantly about whether any woman would find me man enough to marry me and have a family.

Through all the learning of how to do everything again, I never doubted that I would be a good father if given the opportunity. And look at me now. My wife is a good mother and thoughtful wife. We read stories aloud to our kids when they were young. We had this round, green velour loveseat from the seventies, and I can still picture them sitting in it, reading *Heidi*. Michelle loved that book because it had "fancy" gilded edges and a hard cover. Stephen was less interested, but even then he liked the write-your-own-ending books.

They had bedtimes, drank milk with dinner, and understood what good manners were. We took them to museums and theaters and aquariums. We took road trips out west and airplanes to London and ferries to Martha's Vineyard. We camped in tents, even though it was a pain in the ass for me and probably no picnic for Elizabeth either. But these were experiences we'd had as children and wanted to share them with our kids, despite my injury.

I should talk to Michelle. I should talk to Elizabeth. I should talk to Stephen. We need to talk with each other. I don't know where to start. Elizabeth is just so used to turning to other people for support these days that she doesn't realize I'm here in the bedroom, just waiting for her to come in because I need her.

Michelle is angry because we meddled in her life, and now her high school soccer career is over. We told her it could have been worse. Last year, Meagan, one of her good friends, took a school trip to Belize, where she ordered a piña colada from the hotel bar. A chaperone discovered the beverage, and Meagan, an awesome kid, was kicked out of National Honor Society, booted off her softball team, and suspended from her role as student council president and class secretary for thirty school days.

Back when this happened, Michelle loyally defended her friend because she was a great person, the kind of young woman who stood up for others. We agreed with her, but even the best kids can screw up. She knew the rules regarding a school trip. She knew the consequences. She got caught.

Elizabeth shared with Michelle and Stephen that night about a trip she took to Florida on spring break her senior year of high school. She and five friends had driven a minivan to Florida to stay with her aunt. One night, they took a dinner cruise into international waters, and her friend ordered piña coladas just to see if they would be served. The waiter asked to see their IDs, and her friend responded, "Oh, we meant virgin piña coladas, of course." Same situation practically. Elizabeth never would have had the nerve to do that as an individual, but in a group of her peers, she had been far more brazen. She shared the story, hoping to deter our kids from making similar mistakes in which they could get into much more serious trouble.

I think Michelle also realizes that Elizabeth screwed up in not being honest with our family about the embryo adoption. Elizabeth is angry but also guilty for having kept the information from me for so long, so I have that in my favor—as far as the amount of pressure she will put on me to sign.

And Stephen. What is going on in Stephen's head? Why won't he talk to me anymore? I remember him wanting a wheelchair for his tenth birthday. When I asked him why, he just shrugged his shoulders and told people his dad was the coolest person he knew, and he was in a chair, so that was reason enough. Now he has this faraway look on his face as if he desperately wants to tell us something, but he can't make his muscles move his lips to do it.

I need to talk to Elizabeth, and this is one moment when I'm truly cognizant of my wheelchair. How easy it would be to just yell to her down the hall, and I know she would come running. But I need to go to her. I need to make her see that she needs to listen to me. I'm afraid of what's happening to our family. I'm afraid of what's happening to us. I'm afraid of what's happening to me.

I found her in the laundry room, which is handicapped accessible so I can help with the laundry, which I've done a handful of times over the years. So we wouldn't consider laundry a shared chore. Cooking, though, I'm good at. Elizabeth would never fault me for not helping with the meals. I'm not that quick on the cleanup though.

She was doing that crazy kind of laundry sorting that happens when there's a lot to be done. Our kids have been doing their own laundry since they were ten and twelve, I think, so I knew this mess must be all ours. "Can I help?" I gently offered from the hallway, my own kind of apology. She turned and looked up at me, brow furrowed, hair unbrushed and wild, dark circles under her eyes, yet still the most beautiful woman I've ever known.

"I'm just thinking about the follow-up appointment with Stephen's counselor at school. Ms. Hollos really seems to know Stephen better than we do these days, and this makes me feel like a terrible mother. Why has he been so unhappy? What is he hiding from us? He clearly has learned this behavior from watching you and all of your evening escapes." Her glare and frenetic loading of what appeared to be sheets and towels left me unnerved.

"Elizabeth," I said with my voice steady. "I don't know where we went wrong, and if you need to blame me for what is happening, I can handle it. This is not my fault or your fault, but the consequences of a number of decisions we've made along the way. I'm not sure why we're bothering to meet with Ms. Hollos again. Stephen said nothing the last time we met, and the silence was infuriating. Does she know something we don't? The good news is that his grades seem to be improving."

I continued. "The bad news is that he's become even more distant. I thought for sure he would open up to Michelle. If he were doing drugs, Michelle would know, and she definitely would not keep that to herself. She would tell us, right? She would tell you, right?" I needed to hear my wife's reassuring voice telling me that everything was going to be okay. We didn't need to speak of the embryo issue, not then, not till our own kids were in better places.

Elizabeth stopped loading the washing machine, walked toward me, and kneeled down so she was facing me directly, something she did all the time when we were dating. She looked me in the eye and asked, "What would be the one thing Stephen would be afraid to tell you?"

26

Elizabeth

I hated even asking. I knew the answer was not on his radar yet. Stephen is either gay or believes he might be gay. I knew it in my heart, and my heart ached that he felt like he couldn't tell us, whether it had been a long-ago realization or something he had just recently been struggling through. We never talk about homosexuality in this house, not even acknowledging the topic as one in the news.

Andrew promised me all those years ago that he would do his best not to speak badly about the gay lifestyle. He would allow our children to make their own decisions; however, in our silence, we have been in many ways sending the message that homosexuality isn't a topic for discussion in our home, and therefore would not be welcome in our home, period.

Bobby McCarthy was a student in my high school who committed suicide. I remember that we were at basketball practice after school when Adam came running in to tell us Bobby's sister, Laurie, had found him hanging in the garage when she arrived home from school. Laurie was in my class. Bobby was a year behind us, popular, athletic, and smart, seemingly having everything to live for. Their parents were involved in their lives. They came to all of our events. Bobby was loved.

Boys and girls, sobbing together in little clusters, filled the gym. Coaches canceled practice, and we carried our grief home to our families, who hugged us all extra tight, thankful that their kids were safe. Rumors circulated that Bobby might have been gay and that his dad would not accept him. His wake in my hometown was the first I attended. Most of the hundreds of people in attendance were other teenagers like me. I had gone with my basketball team, and we just kept saying how sad that he could have so many friends, yet no one caught on that he was suffering. His parents and sister were broken. His friends would never be the same. His potential for life was gone at fifteen.

I think of Bobby whenever I meet someone with his energy. Andrew's charisma when we first met reminded me of him. I often wondered what Bobby would have grown into had he lived. How had our community failed him? How had no one noticed? Now here is my own son dealing with something equally earth shattering, even if he is not depressed to the point of suicide. He doesn't feel safe coming to us, his parents, with his problems. We've always had an open-door policy and pushed our kids to be honest, but here we are.

Then I think about how old Stephen's soul felt to me, even when he was a baby. We knew, and even Andrew agreed, that Stephen had lived many lives before this one, all of them providing him with the strength and experience to handle adversity and overcome challenges. In this way, he is very much like Andrew. We've always teased Andrew about having come back in this life after losing his last one as a German soldier in World War II, thus explaining his obsession with all things related to that war, Germany, and music from the forties.

I also think about Stephen's early sensitivity for Andrew's wheelchair and him pushing his daddy through parking lots as onlookers both old and young smiled at the sweetness of the scene. I remember him always wanting to help Andrew put his pants on in the morning, and him telling his friends at birthday parties that even though his daddy couldn't walk, he could ride bikes "really fast." He also didn't fight aggressively with his sister like many younger brothers do, as if he knew she would be his only family when Andrew and I were gone.

He truly reveres and admires Michelle and is probably a little jealous of the easier relationship she has always had with her dad because she's extroverted like him. But I'm thinking Stephen has been the wisest among us. He didn't tattle on Michelle or embarrass her at school in front of her peers after the blue tarp incident. He just has an intrinsic sense that Michelle will learn from these experiences and be back on track. Sadly, he apparently can't see that for himself.

As I crouched there in the laundry room and looked into Andrew's eyes, they showed him slowly beginning to understand what I'd asked him. I was reminded of that day we put our embryos up for adoption. If only I had let him say aloud, "I would prefer that our offspring not be raised by two men or two woman." Yet, by not saying it, look where we are. I wished I had told him the babies were born. I wondered how many lives I had lived, and if I could relive this one, what would I do differently?

Andrew never lacked confidence, never lost his smile, even when life was complicated—until now. As he looked back at me from his chair, I imagined he looked like he did when he learned he wouldn't walk again.Z Fear and panic radiated through the laundry room. I held both of his hands, leaned in, and put my head on his chest, a slightly awkward position, given that I needed as many body parts as possible touching his.

"No," he choked quietly, and I felt his heart pounding through his flannel shirt on my forehead.

"Listen to me for one minute," I demanded. "We might not have learned this now if it wasn't for the anger he obviously displayed the night we discussed the embryo adoption and bone marrow consents. This conversation is happening at the exact right time we need it to, Andrew. Who knows what might have happened if he couldn't tell us this, and we couldn't figure it out for ourselves. You love your son. I know this. The fact that he may or may not be gay will not change this about you."

He pushed my hands off and tried to wheel backward out of the hallway and back to his office. "Look at me, goddammit!" I screamed. "Stop! You need to talk through this. You can't talk to Stephen, not now, not like this. He needs to sign those consent forms, and that will be the only forgiveness acceptable to a son who believes his father will not love him when he learns the truth about him."

Andrew did not stop, despite my sobbing pleas. He entered his office and closed the door. I returned to my laundry piles and continued to sort, crying Andrew's name like a child that misses its mother.

27

Michelle

Today is Friday, and I'm officially tired of winter. I need spring and sunlight and warmth besides that from the woodstove.

Mom and Dad are coming to school for another meeting in guidance with Stephen. No one spoke to each other at breakfast. Stephen looked like he was going to throw up. Pretty sure Dad was hung over, because he wouldn't make eye contact with me, nor would he eat any of the scrambled eggs Mom put in front of him. Stephen hopped in my car as opposed to driving in with Mom and Dad.

Tomorrow we will all be swabbed for our bone marrow tests. We know there are at least two fully genetic siblings in the state of New Hampshire. We don't have to be best friends or anything or celebrate Christmas together, but it would be cool to meet, even if our marrow doesn't turn out to be a match. I wonder if they will be like us at all. I wonder who they look like or act like. I wonder what it would be like to have two mothers.

I thought about distracting Stephen with the unknown sibling discussion, but instead decided he was too fragile, based on his pale face and his sweaty hands, which he kept wiping on his jeans.

He was silent in the car. I tried to reach out and touch his hand like Mom used to do when we were little. "It's going to be okay,

Stephen. Be thankful that they care enough to come into school. Believe me, I'm still pissed at them for making me confess to Coach. In the end, of course, I know they did that because they love me, and they don't want to see me make other stupid mistakes that could cost me a job I love or a person I love." I was trying to sound old and wise, but there was a hollowness in my voice I couldn't prevent.

"Stop the car," he demanded.

"Right here? You can't walk to school this far and make it on time, let alone to your meeting with Ms. Hollos. Plus, it's only nine degrees outside. Don't be dumb. What is the worst that can happen?"

He blew up. "How can you be so self-centered? You aren't the only one dealing with shit right now! You are so hell-bent on meeting this other family, the one we are related to, and yet we are so messed up as a family!" he screamed from the passenger seat. "Our father is a paralyzed avoider who hides whiskey and would rather be alone or in a crowd than with our family. Our mother is a control freak who just wants us to look like well-balanced people so that she doesn't have to work so hard at home. You were practically perfect in everyone's eyes until you fucked up, and one mistake gets you kicked off everything, and people still like you. And me, I—I—" His voice trailed off, and he cried quietly, staring out the window.

I let him go on because it was the most he had spoken in months, and frankly I wasn't sure what to say to him. Had he been trying to talk to me? Had he been reaching out, and I'd been too wrapped up with my senior year?

I pulled the car into the parking lot of the Rite Aid, which was still an hour from opening. Leaving the car running, I turned to look at him because the words had stopped flying out of his month. He was just sitting there in the front seat of my beat-up Honda

Prelude, sobbing. The tears raced down his cheeks, and his shoulders shuddered with every breath.

I thought, *Good god, I can't bring him into the building like this. He hasn't cried like this since we had to put our dog down two summers ago.* Edelweiss had been Stephen's best friend. We had grown up together, but she had always been his dog. Sadly, she just got old, stopped eating, and kept trying to run away to the woods to die. We held her in the vet's office as she quieted down and seemingly fell asleep.

I thought, *What if someone sees him, some student who is there early for extra help or to avoid her own sucky home life?* Then it all suddenly made sense: the girl visiting me in my dreams at night, telling me to pay attention to the people I love; the one thing we never talked about in our family beside Dad's accident; the reason Mom didn't tell Dad about the embryo adoption; and the one piece of information Stephen was so desperately afraid to tell Dad and hadn't told me because I always just accepted him being quiet and private. I grabbed his hand and squeezed the hell out of it as I whispered, "They will still love you when you tell them you are gay."

28

Stephen

If I hadn't been crying so hard, I may have attempted to deny her statement, but it felt so good to have it out there in the open, even if open only meant the front seat of her car. "I'm not totally sure I am, but I'm pretty sure. I mean, I don't really have any interest in girls like other guys my age. Why am I telling you this? I think, I just think I'm completely asexual. Please say something, Michelle! I need to know what you're thinking!"

"I'm thinking that I love you, and I'm so sorry you've been feeling so alone with all of this. I'm also thinking that I need to keep driving or our parents are going to send Officer Will looking for us." Officer Will was our school resource officer, whose tattoos often drew students into his office. Michelle asked, "What time is your meeting?"

I told her 7:15, and she slowly pulled back onto the main road. Suddenly, I felt relatively calm, took some deep, cleansing breaths like they teach us in PE, and then wiped my face with my shirttail. I didn't want to think about Dad right then. Ms. Hollos assured me that he loves me, and that he'd accept this news even if it took him a little while to get used to it.

What's the worst that can happen? I wondered.

I was sure Michelle was thinking about how she could pull Dad aside before the meeting to soften the blow, to remind him how much he loves me, etc. I'm seventeen years old. I knew I should be able to handle this better, but my worst fear was that he would just roll out of the room and not look me in the eye. At least Mom insisted that they drive to school together; I couldn't imagine he would leave her at school if he needed to escape. Worst-case scenario, I decided, was Dad running off and leaving Mom in the guidance office, and her yelling, "I want a divorce!" I didn't need my possible gayness to break up the family. If that didn't happen, then we could be okay.

I thought about telling Michelle this, as we'd clearly broken the vulnerability barrier. I decided instead to confide with her about my new pen pal. "You remember how I intercepted the mail from the social worker? Then the one from the two mothers requesting we be tested? Well, we received another letter, only this one was written by Caroline's twin brother, Brian. It was an amazing letter, and I think Dad would be onboard with the marrow testing if he read it, so I brought it with me. My thought was, if my meeting got too intense, or I bailed out of telling the truth yet again, I could always fire away, reading this to Mom and Dad. It would be like saying no to a person's face, and he could never do that. Especially because this kid, his name is Brian, sounds so much like Dad, well, I guess even a male version of you. He is funny, even considering his sister being so sick.

"When I say he sounds like Dad, I mean he sounds like the younger, happier version of Dad, the person he is when he is at a social event or there are a lot of friends at the house, and he is trying to entertain or make people laugh. I'm not like that. I am a good person. I am nice and smart and handsome, but people aren't attracted to me like they are to you, and him, and probably to this guy, Brian.

You know I have a few good friends at school, but we are more quiet people. We play our music together, and we just don't talk that much."

"So, can I ask you a question?" she asked as we pulled into a parking spot at school.

"You just did," I replied, my lame attempt at humor.

"Is there someone you're interested in at school, someone who has made this such a big deal this year?"

"Wouldn't this be a big deal regardless of what year? Or what time of year? I think for a long time I just thought I was awkward around girls, and that's why I didn't learn to flirt with them when everyone else did. Then in ninth grade, I realized that made me look a little weird, so I would ask girls to dance with me at functions. Then last year, when Becky really liked me, and I didn't like her back the same way, I realized I couldn't pretend. This year—wait. To answer your question, there isn't one specific person I like; I was just feeling like a fraud, lying to myself, and I was angry because Mom and Dad never made it seem like it would be acceptable if I was gay. They don't even mention the word, for God's sake."

"Are you okay to go inside?" Michelle asked. "Do you want me to come with you? You know I'm happy to do that. I'm really just glad you told me before you told them."

"It's not a competition, Michelle, and I think I'll be all right without you. Ms. Hollos is awesome, and she'll talk me through the whole thing, and I already played the worst-case scenario over in my head, so it shouldn't be too bad. I'm going to give Dad the letter, so he can think about it this afternoon. Tomorrow, we should all go and be swabbed. I did a little research online, and none of it is invasive. They don't even need to take any blood if you don't pass the first screening. And if none of us is a match, I think we should write back or call Brian to say we tried."

"Sounds like a plan. Now you take your gay self right on in there!" She smiled, and I couldn't help but do the same. When smiles are a long time in between, I remember every one.

As I walked to the guidance office, I heard my own personal anthem playing in my head. First it was the classic *Rocky* theme song, when Rocky was training on the steps of the Philadelphia Art Museum. I remembered racing Michelle up those steps as a kid when we visited, and feeling guilty Dad couldn't climb the steps with us. He waited patiently at the bottom, smiling.

The next song flashed through, another classic from my parents' generation, "Eye of the Tiger." I felt as if I needed a coach to shake down my shoulders to loosen me up moments before being put in the game for the play of my life. I felt myself sweating, my heart pumping, but I was ready. Mom and Dad were waiting for me outside Ms. Hollos's office.

"Son, we were worried." Dad touched my hand, and I knew he knew.

"You and Michelle left before us," explained Mom. "And her car wasn't in the front lot when we arrived."

Ms. Hollos opened her door, smiled, and beckoned us into the office. I looked into my dad's face, and he was looking directly into my eyes. I knew it would be okay.

When we were all sitting down on Ms. Hollos's comfy guidance counselor furniture, I shut the "Coming out to your parents" soundtrack down in my mind, and I opened my mouth to speak, not even needing Ms. Hollos's introduction.

But suddenly Dad burst into tears. "We love you, son, and no matter what you need to tell us, we will still love you."

I looked out the window, watching the snow fall quietly and feeling my throat choke up, not because of being afraid of how my parents would respond, but because this was the vulnerable side of my dad I had never seen before. Maybe we were more alike than I thought.

"I'm not sure completely, but I need you to know that I might be gay."

29

Jessie

I'm thinking that it wasn't a good idea, but his voice was so compelling. It could make the difference between life and death.

We finally heard from the family—well, the son actually. His name is Stephen, and he is a junior in high school. His sister is a senior. As a family, they're driving to Portsmouth to meet us for lunch, and then they would like to meet Caroline in the hospital. He called Brian last week, and together they made a plan. The father, Andrew, has been the hold-out, but Stephen is confident he will do the right thing and be tested before leaving the hospital.

Stephen sounded like a great kid, young man, young adult, very poised, confident, everything a parent wants their child to grow into. How is it possible for one of his parents to be afraid of gay people? I need to stop saying *afraid*, because, for some people, it's not fear at all, but rather a fundamental belief structure.

I try not to put myself in harm's way, so this little luncheon could totally backfire, but Brian has assured me the man is professional, disabled even, so that should make him more compassionate, right? Well, I've been wrong before.

Brian also told me that within the last few weeks Stephen came out to his family that he believed he was gay. Poor kid. That must have been exceedingly difficult for him to come out to parents he knew were only 50 percent supportive. It's amazing how much this news has taken my mind off of Caroline's cancer. I can't stop thinking about how I will greet this young man. Will I hug him, or would that be too weird? A handshake doesn't seem like enough. Nor would a fist pound be appropriate.

Not every gay person's experience is the same, obviously, but I'm suddenly thrown back to 1987, when I first came out to my friends, who claimed they already knew. The hardest person to tell was my boyfriend at the time, mostly due to the constant barrage of jokes he endured from his friends, saying that he had "turned me gay." Telling my parents was also hard because I was a freshmen in college; but because of how liberal and accepting they were, they chalked it up to me being "experimental." They wore my gay identity like a badge or a silk scarf or a new pinned-up accessory. "This is our daughter, Jessie, and she is gay!" I imagined that they heard a pep band playing in the background as the announcer came on. "And starting at midfield today, is Jessie Woodland, and she is gaaayyyyy!" Or better yet, around the holidays in superloud voices, "And you remember Jessie's partner, Allison? Well, they were *married* in a *civil union* just this last summer. Isn't it all wonderful?"

When we started talking about raising a family, my dad had it in his head that we would both just try to have sex with a man "the old-fashioned way." In fact, I believe his words were "It was good enough for our generation; it should be good enough for yours—and a whole lot cheaper than all of that fertility crap!" So we decided not to tell them anything about not using our own eggs. That way, they would ask fewer questions.

Once those babies arrived, it didn't matter whose they were biologically; what mattered was that they were ours and that all the grandparents, despite having been raised in a different time and place, were accepting of our becoming parents in the first place. As much as we miss our parents, I am thankful that they have been spared seeing their granddaughter be on the verge of dying and helpless to do anything. Our kids all have wonderful memories of them; all were avid skiers and swimmers and shared summer vacations on Lake Winnipesaukee or the coast of Maine.

I can't help but imagine the worst of these people we are about to meet for lunch; yet we chose them all those years ago for their prime set of embryos. In a matter of hours, we will be meeting them for Mexican food; at least we all agreed on that. Now, if we can only persuade Andrew to let his son be swabbed. I have a feeling *he* is, ironically, the answer to our prayers.

30

Allison

I'm sitting in the car, having left work early to meet Jessie and Brian for lunch with the Embryo Family. I promised myself I wouldn't call them that—Brian's name for them, really—and here I go. Brian feels really good about their son, Stephen, and I can already sense he is getting his hopes up about this supercool, urban-hip, blended family—*after* saving his sister's life, of course. Despite his maturity and agelessness, he really is only fifteen. Yet when I look back at the last five months or so since Caroline's diagnosis, it has been Brian who has held our family together. His sense of humor and strength have never wavered.

How does he maintain this optimism throughout what has been the worst year of our life? Just the other day, we were at the pharmacy, refilling one of Caroline's prescriptions, which rang up to close to $100, and his response was "We should be grateful for our health insurance. Imagine what it would cost." What freshman in high school talks about being grateful for health insurance?

There was a knock at my window, and it was Brian, his face smiling and handsome. I'm such a coward. I was really wanting to arrive late, so that the awkward introductions could already have been made, and I could just slide into my seat and enter into the conversation. But Brian, oh Brian, he felt it was important to enter as a family unit, so that Stephen's parents could see just that: a family unit. Yet where would we be if Brian hadn't written that incredibly beautiful and poignant letter asking them to consider his sister? Saying no to him truly is impossible.

"Are you waiting for something?" he asked, grinning, and I begrudgingly opened my door.

"Just wanted to make sure we walk in as a family unit," I reminded him. Of course, he had thought to make a reservation, so there were our seven seats around a lovely table in the corner. The Embryo Family had not arrived yet.

"Moms," Brian cautioned, "just relax, and don't be weird."

"Define *weird*," I replied, catching on to his demeanor. "Are we allowed to order a cocktail for this event?" I was serious in my question; I had not felt so much stress in meeting someone in years.

"No, you can't order a cocktail! We don't even know if they drink. I mean, one doesn't even like gay people, so let's keep our wits about us, shall we?" He had definitely taken over the role of parent. I even imagined him facilitating the greetings, with him saying something similar to "So good of you to join us here to discuss your homophobia along with saving my sister's life. And, by the way, isn't it weird that you are our biological parents, and you are our brother and sister? What should we order for lunch?"

Throughout the process of adopting the embryos who would later reach their potential of life to become our children, I was the one most afraid of the long-term ethical questions. Jessie just knew that it would all work out, and Brian would never fall in love his senior year of college with his biological sister who just happened to be at grad school; nor would Caroline one day meet her brother in a coed softball league years after college and fall in love with him.

My worst nightmare: either one of them bringing a special friend home to meet the parents and us thinking that their physical appearances could turn into something far more complex: I'm sorry, but you're going to need to take a blood test to date our daughter. You know, just to rule out the fact that you may or may not be her brother. Or worse: I know this must seem like a strange question, but did your parents use any fertility assistance through Dartmouth Hitchcock Medical Center—*ever?*

Being lesbian parents would be the least weird thing about us, and there was Brian telling us to try not to be weird. This whole thing was bizarre, and if we could have done it differently, we would have. Or would we? Then we wouldn't have the Brian and Caroline we have now, and we wouldn't be trying to save Caroline's life.

Thankfully, I didn't have to think much longer, because Brian stood up from his chair to greet this family who had already forever changed our lives. I watched the words come from Brian's lips: "You must be Mr. and Mrs. Walker. So good to meet you. My name is Brian, and these are my mothers, Jessie and Allison." I stood to shake their hands.

31

Brian

The mother grabbed me in this ridiculous bear hug. So much for the days of stranger danger. "Thank you so much for your letter," she said. From my moments on the phone with Stephen, I didn't think the family would be huggers at all, but clearly they were, except for the father. He looked pale and sickly, and I was doubting it had anything to do with being in a wheelchair.

The odd thing was, when I shook Stephen's hand and then accepted his hug, I felt as if we had known each other for years, which is impossible, since we had only just met that very instant. He didn't look anything like me, but I did look like the woman who sat across the table from me. The whole thing was really too crazy, if one thought about it for too long.

When Moms first told me how we were born, I thought very much in terms of science and test tubes and petri dishes. As a little kid, I didn't think much about it at all, but, probably by age nine, I had started asking my first questions about in vitro fertilization. I understood there was an egg and some sperm, and they fertilized the egg outside of the woman's body and then put it back inside. In my situation, I was frozen for two years! Two years!

At around ten or eleven, I really wondered if there could be long-term side effects from being frozen for so long before being born, but Moms reassured me that plenty of research had been done, blah, blah, blah. I have always believed that is one reason I try so hard at school but don't want to look like I'm trying so hard. No one is going to accuse me of being a few cells short of a complete human being just because I was on ice, frozen in time for two years before birth.

So if this man sitting across from me, next to Stephen, was the sperm part of my embryo and hers was the egg part, they must have really wanted children badly to spend all that money. As I think about Moms in the same way, it seems unfair that some people just have to think about getting pregnant—and in some cases, there is no thought at all—and, whammo, they're pregnant. Then there are all of those teenagers or people just barely into their twenties who can barely take care of themselves, let alone a baby—double whammo. They are often not developmentally mature enough or financially ready to be independent from their own parents.

Yet there we sat, at a lovely table on a sunny day, the adults all desperately looking like they could use an alcoholic drink but believing that would send the wrong message. Whereas the young folk at the table looked like they'd better run the conversation. I guess if one grows up with a dad in a wheelchair or lesbians for mothers, neither family is traditional in any sense.

Michelle cleared her throat to begin. *Wow, the daughter takes control of the situation. Impressive. Maybe we are more alike than I thought.*

I wanted to blurt out across table, "Please save my sister. She is your sister too, and you would love her like we do." But the last thing I wanted to do was appear desperate. I also thought Moms were a little worried I might secretly fall in love with this other, only slightly more "normal" family.

I've tried to explain whenever the annual request comes up for us to see a family therapist to deal with the "adolescent issues that may arise from having lesbian mothers" that really it's not that strange. I don't need a male father figure in the sense that everyone thinks I need one. I have plenty of dad-like figures in my life: my uncles, male friends of Moms, male teachers, my drama/comedy club coach. They all look out for me, probably even more than they do for an average male high school student, because I guess I'm what they call "at risk." Ironically, this kid, Stephen, is growing up in a middle-class family with a mother and a father, and neither one of them is gay, and both of them stopped paying enough attention to recognize he was really hurting.

"Thank you for sending your letter to our family," Michelle said. "My dad is ready to be swabbed, and Stephen went yesterday when Dad signed off on the consents. They are going to fax over the results today to see if he is a match. I'm a preliminary match, but they will do further blood work when we get to the hospital." I watched her as she spoke, composed, clearly a little embarrassed by her father's behavior but proud enough not to apologize. They were there, and that would have to be enough. Before I had a chance to reply, both my mothers were crying and blubbering, "Thank you, thank you," and trying to embrace this man and woman and their children all at once.

I felt compelled to remind them that even though these were two more people to be tested, we should not put all our hopes into this. They could still not be a match, and we would be back to square one again. Why I always have to be the voice of reason is beyond me.

Andrew softly said, "I'm sorry it took me longer to reply. Both Elizabeth and I have siblings, and they have children, so there are more people to test if needed. I've spoken to both of our families, and everyone is willing to be tested right away, and we will do whatever is needed to help your daughter. I'm really hoping I'm the one who is the match; since I can't feel half my body, the procedure will be painless for me."

This made us all laugh, and the discomfort surrounding Andrew's initial distaste of our family was broken. He cleared his throat and started again. "This really has less to do with the fact that you are lesbians and more with the fact that I'm overwhelmed by the idea that, after my spinal cord injury, I was so worried about whether I could become a father. We were thrilled with having our own two kids, and although I understood the possibility of other babies being born by donating our embryos, it's a little like someone coming by your home and saying, 'Oh, wait, you forgot about these two.' Only we don't have to be responsible for these other lives. But now, in a way we do, because we know they exist and that they need us. Like good parents, we want to be there when we're needed, and I've learned only recently how very important that is."

Before the conversation could go on any longer, Mom's phone rang; it was Caroline's nurse reporting that the infection she had developed earlier in the week had escalated. They needed to put her into a drug-induced coma to help her fight off the infection with superstrong antibiotics. At that point, she was too sick to risk a bone marrow transplant, even if all the Walkers were matches.

We immediately said good-bye to each other, not having ordered our food. To their credit, the Walkers told us they would find us at the hospital. If I could have driven us there myself, I would have, because neither mom was in any shape to drive. This was the sickest Caroline had ever been, and no one seemed to hold out much hope that she could pull this one off. But I knew my sister, and if she knew what lay ahead, she would not give up easily.

32

Caroline

I have an infection. The nurses explained they were going to use a drug to put me into a state where my body could rest to fight it off. If they couldn't get a handle on the infection, I would never be able to survive a bone marrow transplant, even if they did find a donor match.

This is an odd experience; there are times when I feel like I'm floating over my own body sleeping in the hospital bed. People scurry around, attending to other patients, eating their lunches quickly in the cafeteria, communicating to families like mine what is happening with their children or other loved ones. I wish I could reach out to Moms and "use my words" to tell them it's all going to be okay. Intuitively, I know this. I feel it in every limb and cell of my body.

Between these moments of lucid tranquility, various characters in good books I've read visit me. And there are some other young people standing in the back of the hospital room just listening, which is so weird. Yet, while it's happening, it feels completely normal.

One of the strangers looks familiar, and I have a distant memory of eating a giant chocolate ice cream cone with sprinkles with her and walking down a busy road. Then there were sirens and many people crying. Another girl is wearing a punk-rock purple wig and looks at me as if she understands exactly what I'm feeling lying here sick in a hospital bed. She whispers to me that she knows my hair will grow back, and I will get well again.

One of the boys in the back doesn't say anything at all but has the most compassionate eyes I've ever seen. He reaches for my hand, and I let him hold it because I can tell it makes him feel better. When his fingers clasp my own, I see his family of sisters and one brother crying over a casket, and somehow I know it's Mother's Day.

The other boy is standing on the outside of the window, making funny faces at us in the room, and we all smile. I have a memory him dancing inside a pizza place in front of a large glass window, where we watched from the outside, sitting in a car. Then I remember his mother trying to wake him up, and she thinks he's playing a game because he was always playing games. But in this memory, he doesn't wake up, and I know it's still Mother's Day. These faces are so familiar, but they don't fit exactly into the life I live now. It's as if I'm transported to another lifetime.

This all seems so sad, yet I know they are here to help me. Then they move back to make room for the others coming around my bed. I realize the new visitors are my favorite characters from books I've read. Like a little while ago, Scout from *To Kill a Mockingbird* showed up and asked, "Whatcha doing?" as if we were old friends. She told me all about Boo Radley, Tom Robinson, and what a good man her father is, even if he does want her to "act more like a lady."

We talked about when bad things happen to good people— and even in the eyes of the law—because people let their emotions take charge of their reasons, and it all gets confusing. She said it's great being a character in a book, because she will never have to grow up. Like Peter Pan, she'll always live in childhood, even if she learns some hard lessons in that childhood about the way people treat one another. Glancing around the room, the girl with the ice cream, the boy with the complex eyes, the girl with the purple wig, and the boy with the smile all nod knowingly.

While she continued to chat, Ophelia opened the door—the version of Ophelia before she drowns herself over Hamlet rejecting her. If only Ophelia had been able to meet a Scout or a Jane Eyre or the more contemporary Hermione. Or even the badass Mulan—not the one from the Disney movie, although I did love that as a kid, but the real Mulan from that wicked old poem, or ballad maybe, where she replaces her father in war and destroys evil all over and returns home a hero who is actually discovered to be a heroine. Love that, even though I despise violence in all forms.

No, characters like Ophelia and Gatsby's Daisy and Scarlett O'Hara have nothing on spunky Charlotte from *Charlotte's Web* and, my all-time favorite, Margaret from *Are You There God, It's Me, Margaret.* And the fact that Jane Austen wrote *Pride and Prejudice* when she was just twenty-one is utterly amazing.

I'd be lying if I pretended I hadn't read all the Nancy Drew series between ages eight and eleven. In fact, I found the first one in the basement of a church in a little village called Chesuncook on a camping trip in Maine with Moms years ago. The book was at least forty years old and smelled of mold and mildew, yet I couldn't wait to find out what happened next. Who would Nancy save? What mystery would she solve? The series that came next was *Anne of Green Gables*, and I desperately dreamed of being a redheaded orphan.

Suddenly, Margaret is next to my bed, talking about God. I'm not sure I believe in God either, and I probably should be praying to someone to get better. But she says it for me, quoting from the book, "We're moving today. I'm so scared, God. I've never lived anywhere but here. Suppose I hate my new school? Suppose everyone there hates me? Please help me, God. Don't let New Jersey be too horrible. Thank you." And then she just stands there looking at me. She's wearing her long, brown hair straight down either side of her face, purple shorts, black kneesocks, and a striped shirt. I know she's only in sixth grade, but she seems way older. Margaret must be one of those old souls too, even though she's just a character in a story published in 1970. Timeless. Classic. Universal. It's what makes the good ones stay good.

I remember my teacher, Mr. Thompson, wrote a play about characters from classic literature meeting each other. We thought it was weird, but it's not nearly as weird as this experience is. I know I'm not awake, but I feel such friendship with these souls surrounding me. Characters in books become real people too, just as these other souls, the ones I recognize and can't place, must have been with me in other places—other lives maybe? I need to remember this when I wake up so I can write about it.

I ask the congregation surrounding me the hospital room if they would pray for me, and they circle around my bed, holding hands. Although I know none of it is real, this is the most peace I've felt in a very long time. I feel as if I need to speak to them, tell them something, since they are here supporting me. "So, this young adult author came to our school last year. His name was Matt de la Peña, and I loved his books, all of them, even though none of them had a strong female protagonist, which I generally go for. I think the reason I wanted to read his books so badly had to do with what he said about characters. He told our class while we were talking about how he got the ideas for his books that when a writer creates a new character, he or she first has to imagine what kind of person the character is. Would he be someone who would hold the door open for a stranger? Would she be someone you would want to have a picnic with? What would he pack for lunch? Egg salad or fried chicken or turkey wrap?

What are her flaws? No one wants to read about a perfect character or an insecure character. What do you think about that, Margaret?"

Before Margaret could answer, Scout pushed her way back through the literary soul circle, offered me a Twix bar, and said she'd found it at the nurse's station. I think it's time I wake up.

33

Andrew

The hospital didn't allow us to see Caroline due to her critical condition, but I completed the swab test, and Michelle had further blood work done. We will know those results tomorrow, but regardless, Caroline will need a few days to recover from the infection completely to get her ready for the bone marrow transplant.

We drove home as a family, and conversation was limited, as it had been a draining day for all of us. Since everything had happened with the "sibs," as Michelle had nicknamed Caroline and Brian, life seemed less catastrophic, but certainly not settled.

But I couldn't settle down for the night until after Stephen and I had a much-needed conversation. I knocked on his bedroom door, wanting to respect his privacy but also desperately needing him to allow my entrance into his safe space. Sadly, I could not remember the last time I had crossed the threshold into his upstairs bedroom.

When the kids were younger, it just took too long to get up there, due to having to take the chair lift upstairs, which broke down periodically. As they grew up, not going upstairs just became a pattern of life. We always ate dinner as a family, and both kids always came downstairs to watch TV, read books, or play Uno after their homework was done. On the rare occasion, Stephen brought friends by the house. Today, I fired up the old chair lift because I needed to say what I needed to say in a place that kept Stephen safe. I needed to tell him my darkest secret and hope that it would make sense to him.

"Please open the door, Buddy. We need to talk," I pleaded gently. I heard his giant feet pad toward the door, and I imagined him taking a deep breath, wanting to avoid the conversation about to be had, whatever it would entail.

He opened the door wearing my brother's old Connecticut College sweatshirt. My brother, Scott—the one who went to college, became a stockbroker, did everything right—lives in New Jersey. He has always been good to Stephen and understood his quietness. He accompanied us on many a camping and fishing trip to Maine. He would be happy to know that Stephen was still rocking his old, worn-out CC sweatshirt.

"Hey, Dad, what are you doing upstairs?" he asked.

"We need to talk, Stephen. Actually, I need to talk, and you need to listen. You don't need to say anything, but I'm happy to answer any of your questions." I paused. "That is a lie. I won't be happy to answer them, but I will work hard to explain, because there's nothing happy about what I'm going to tell you."

"Jesus, Dad, you really know how to break the ice," he said with a smile as he opened the door all the way. After about two years of living in this house, Elizabeth's brother, Jeff, covered from head to toe in tattoos and piercings, had widened the doorway. Then we repainted the hallway together. What a disaster that was! Elizabeth insisted on helping to paint and just about put Jeff over the edge. She is amazing at many things, but painting isn't one of them.

Stephen picked up a few articles of clothing strewn on the floor so I didn't wheel over them. He had always been a fastidious kid, so I was a little surprised his clothes weren't put away. Not knowing exactly how long this was going to take, because I had never told anyone the story, I transferred out of my wheelchair into the overstuffed chair in the corner, which had been my father's. A few weeks after Dad's death, Stephen decided the chair needed to come home to his bedroom. He had fond memories of climbing into Grampy's lap and reading books with him or listening to his record collection.

Stephen sat down on the edge of his bed, only slightly rumpled and covered with sheets of music and some pencils.

"You working on something?" I asked.

"Yeah, I haven't been creative in a while. Juniors can perform an original piece at the spring concert, which I would like to do, but first I have to conduct one piece for Mr. Clermont to show I'm capable. So, I decided I better get going on it, since spring has almost arrived."

"When is the concert?"

"May twentieth, and I'd like you and Mom to be there if you aren't traveling," he declared.

I'm not sure if him wanting me there or him about to be a senior or him composing his own music brought tears to my eyes. I knew this would be harder than I thought. "Listen, if I don't tell you this now, I'll lose my courage. But I'm not proud of what I have to tell you. This is the biggest mistake of my life."

"Bigger than breaking into that liquor store in high school?"

"Yes, way bigger than that." I couldn't help smiling at his need for a comparison.

"When I was your age, one of my buddies lived down the street and had since we were little kids. We built tree forts together and defended the younger kids against the neighborhood bully. We tried to sail a homemade raft down the Merrimack River like Huck Finn and Tom Sawyer but ended up crashing it, almost sinking, and walking five miles home. This was before the days of cell phones, mind you.

"His parents were divorced, and he lived with his mom and didn't have any brothers or sisters. His mom worked two jobs to pay their bills, and he had to spend a lot of time by himself, which is why he was at our house so much. It was the late seventies, early eighties, and people didn't worry about their kids playing outside, and we wouldn't have been allowed to watch the television or play endless video games like kids now. The woods were our best entertainment."

I glanced over at him, sitting cross-legged on his bed like he would when he was seven, enraptured by a tale I was telling him. "In middle school, Chris didn't have as many friends at school as I did, but we ate lunch together every day and rode the bus and often hung out at my house after school. Then I started playing school sports, and he chose not to, so we drifted apart a little bit. In high school, we still had band together, and he was involved in drama; he starred in the school musical. We were best friends, really, and one night—God this is hard, Stephen."

"Dad," he said, "you're killing me with this buildup. What the hell happened? You've never mentioned a Chris before. What happened?!"

"One night we were watching a movie, and he tried to open up to me. I remember the popcorn being ridiculously buttery and taking a sip of Fresca. He asked me if I ever worried about what people thought of me. We were in ninth grade, and of course I cared deeply about what people thought about me. I told him I avoided saying things out loud if I thought anyone would think it weird.

"Then he asked if he and I would be friends forever, which I thought was weird for one of my guy friends to ask. But I was trying to reassure him, even though our friendship had already changed a lot

128

since elementary school. So I just said that even when we were busy, I would always make time for him if he needed a friend.

"'Really?' he said, like he was surprised, and then, 'Can I ask you something personal?' At the time, I didn't think too much about it, and said, 'Of course,' thinking he was going to tell me about a girl he liked or something going on with his mom at home.

"Let me add something. Being around Chris always made me feel more secure. I felt like I was the older brother, or I was the one who had better luck with friends, teachers, or girl stuff. Deep down, I hoped Chris would always be in my life, since he was my oldest friend, and he understood me when I went off on a rant or was embarrassed at school by something. I could say anything in front of Chris and never worry about the repercussions or what other people thought. He was the one person, beside my family, I could be myself around. And then he—he—grabbed my hand."

"What? What do you mean, he grabbed your hand? Like he was holding it?"

"I freaked out, Stephen. I'm sure he was just trying to connect with me, but I thought he was going to try to kiss me or something. I shoved him and told him to get the fuck out of my house. I didn't know enough then, Stephen. I didn't know he was just trying to tell me that he needed me to listen. I'm not proud of what I did next, but I told him I didn't want to be friends with a faggot. More importantly, I was worried about what people would think about me if they knew I was friends with him."

I watched Stephen stand and slowly back away from me, but there was nowhere he could go without jumping over this bed. "I know it wasn't right, but I was confused too. I was angry that it seemed like he was taking advantage of our friendship, making it so easy to be around him, and I was nervous about what that would say about me. I wished Chris could be around more with my other friends, because I liked the way he made me feel. Did that or would that make me gay too? I know this is awful to hear, especially considering what you've been going through, but this is exactly why I need to tell you."

"Dad, in this moment, I hate you. I'm sure I will get over it, but why would you think he was going to kiss you? He needed you to be his friend. And how did you treat him? Like an asshole! I guess I'm lucky not to have friends like you. Chris trusted you, and he thought you trusted him."

"Let me finish. He was someone that I would see around school, but, after that day at the house, I never made eye contact with him again. One day after PE, we were in the locker room, getting changed, and someone brought up that Chris might be gay. Now, remember this was the mid-eighties, when most people believed that gay people and drug users caused and spread the AIDS epidemic. There was so much fear surrounding that term: *gay*. We had never talked about it in our family at home, so when the other guys started trashing Chris for being gay, I never defended him.

"Even if he was gay, I should have been strong enough to say, 'He's a great guy; we've been friends since elementary school.' I should have told them the story about when he kicked a kid's ass for throwing me down. I should have told them that he helped me stack wood when that was my primary winter chore, and he didn't even want me to share my allowance.

"I should have said, 'What's the big deal?' The thing is, it was a big deal. A very big deal. I didn't even ask them what made them think that. Back then, very few kids were out that they were gay, especially in high school.

"So there are two things. One, I'm very proud of you for having the confidence to say who you are, even if you're afraid of how you will be accepted. You are an incredibly strong man to be able to do that, way stronger than your dad was at your age."

"Chris and I sound an awful lot alike," he said. "We both needed your approval. Well, what happened to Chris?"

That was the question I had feared most.

"That's the second thing, Stephen. By not standing up for Chris, I might as well have condemned him to death. Suddenly, I found myself on the other side of our friendship. Instead of saying hi and smiling when I passed him in the hallway, I turned the other way; I ignored him. I never went as far as shoving him or calling him names like some of the other guys, but I'm just as guilty for not reaching out and being a friend.

"You know how Greg and I became friends in high school? He actually understood how sad that made me, but even he said, 'Don't worry so much about it; he has his own people now.' Only then did it occur to me that Chris probably thought I had spread the rumor about him being gay. I had ruined him without even meaning to. Scott was already off at college, and I didn't really trust anyone else with how to handle it."

"Dad, I don't have a good feeling about this. What happened to him?" Stephen had begun to perspire.

"Son, he never deserved what happened to him. All I know is that spring of our junior year had been hell for him. One day, he was at school, and the next day he wasn't. I should have called his mother or stopped by the house, because he was never absent, and I had a sick feeling. Instead, my mother asked another neighbor about Chris. He had committed suicide. He turned his car on in the garage and died from carbon-monoxide poisoning. Chris's mom found him when she came home from work. The neighbor, Mrs. Cooper, had heard her screams, but it was too late. He had been gone several hours. He had probably done it in the morning right after she had left for work.

"There was a note. He wanted the world to know that he was not gay, if it mattered that much, but that he was completely alone in the world, and his mom would be better off without a loser like him in the house. I will never forget those words. They replayed over and over again in my head for days … for weeks … for months. I went to his funeral with my parents and siblings to pay our respects, but I was ashamed. My own parents were so sad and perplexed by his suicide, and I felt partially responsible for not being the friend he thought I could be to him.

"His poor mother was simply in shock. She hugged each of us and thanked us for remembering Chris as a happy boy from our childhood. Clearly, Chris had not told her how I had treated him those last few years. Selfishly, I was so worried about how she would look at me, I didn't even think about how she had lost everything that truly mattered."

"Dad, I can't believe you could do that to someone? I've always thought you were this superhero of a man, the guy who could conquer anything, the guy who could survive losing the use of his legs—he could do anything. But you aren't much of man at all. Does Mom know this story? She can't know, or she never would have married you."

"I know, son. I'm not proud of my part in this. No, she doesn't know this story. It's more important now than ever that you know this about your father. I want you to understand that I will spend the rest of my life trying to make up for this mistake."

"Only because your son has just come out. How long would you have kept that bottled up inside? It's no wonder you sneak away to your room to drink in secret. I would too if I'd done something that shameful."

"That's the worst of it, but there are other consequences. The night of my accident"—I heard my voice getting soft because I'd never told anyone this either—"we weren't horsing around in the car, although that's what we said we were doing. Kevin, the asshole I should never have been friends with, made a snide comment about the fact that I hadn't gone all the way with a girl. He said this in front of Greta, my date for prom, sitting next to me in the passenger seat. Then he joked that maybe I was gay and that my fag boyfriend had offed himself last spring."

"Oh, Dad."

"I went crazy, trying to hit him from the front seat. Saying I was gay was far worse than anything anyone could have called me. Plus, it stirred up the guilt and shame I had felt over Chris's suicide. Unfortunately, my temper got the best of me, and the next thing I remember, I was waking up two weeks later and learning that I was paralyzed.

"Two things happened during my coma. One was that Kevin and the girls in the car, when they thought I was going to die, promised never to tell anyone how the accident really happened. And two, Chris's mother stopped by the hospital to drop off a poster that had been Chris's that she thought I would want. It's that poster of the Justice League of superheroes that hangs in my office. It hung on the wall across from my hospital bed, then followed me to my rehab stint and then home to my bedroom. I imagined those superheroes were Chris and me, and we would conquer the world if he was still living.

"I made enormous mistakes that played a role in a really great kid taking his own life, simply because I was a coward. I shut that part of my life off and never spoke of it again because, until now, being gay was the worst thing I could be accused of. However, I'm so ashamed of the way I allowed you, one of three people I would trade my life for, to feel so unfairly treated. And to think you were afraid to come to me with this same issue is equally shameful. I'm so very sorry, Stephen."

"Dad, I don't know what to say," is all that comes out of my mouth. But my mouth is filled with so many words I want to hurl at the world. At him. At the 17 year old version of him. At the old man version of him. Everything. What he has told me is almost unforgivable. I'm sure Chris wasn't even gay. I bet he needed to trust that he could be vulnerable with you. It's crazy to me that someone who could be so smart could be so dumb. That story is way worse than breaking into a liquor store. I'd like to say to him, "Since you are here for me now, that matters more than anything." But I can't. I can't say that yet. But in my heart, I think if Chris was here now, he would forgive my dad, both the man he has become and the boy he once was.

I replied, "It doesn't matter if he was gay or not; what matters is that when my friend needed me the most, I pushed him away—just like I was pushing you away, my own son. I was a coward and thought that if I held his hand, I might be gay too. Chris was my oldest friend, and my betrayal cost him his life. I loved Chris, and I was nervous those feelings could turn into something more. The same mistake almost cost me my son." Then I asked him the worst question a parent could ever want an answer to. "Stephen, did you ever think about ending your life?"

He stood there arms crossed, defensive, absorbing the question slowly. He tilted his head, as if tasting the words in his mouth before saying, "I think that for someone to end their life, there has to be more going on inside than just feeling unaccepted. I've been depressed, sure, and feeling sorry for myself for being different from what I know you hoped for me, but I didn't want to die. Fortunately, even when you and Mom didn't notice the changes, people at school did. Cam is a good friend, and he told Ms. Hollos he was worried about me. My teachers paid attention too and reached out to make sure I knew they were there. There's a lot you can do to make up for our lost time and the time you lost with Chris. I love you, Dad."

"I love you too, son," I told him.

And I'm crying, mostly because my boy, the one who used to dress as Spiderman, wear a cape to bed, and carry a shield while riding his bicycle, has grown up into a stronger man than I could ever be.

34

Elizabeth

Thinking back on the two big events of the week, which one made the biggest difference to me? Does it matter?

Just yesterday, we met another part of our life. Just a few days before that, we sat in Ms. Hollos's office with Stephen as he bravely shared with us that he thought he was gay. I'm not sure what he was expecting to happen, for the walls to implode or for his father's head to fly off or for us to bolt from the office. None of that happened, perhaps because we already knew and needed to support him through saying the words. Andrew wheeled to Stephen and leaned over for a hug. They both cried. I cried. I'm fairly certain Ms. Hollos cried. I wonder how many times she has witnessed a teen in crisis due to depression or drug addiction or abandonment or even this, a need to out himself to the world.

When Stephen finally pulled away from the embrace his father wasn't quite ready to release, I reached over, held his hand, and smiled. I'm thankful he's living today and not twenty or thirty years ago, when it would have been much harder for him to face his parents. It's easier for us too, since we know he can still live a successful life and be happy and not feel like he has to hide away from the world; although I regret we let him do just that in his bedroom with his music for the past year.

Relief filled the room, as did some awkward moments. "What happens now?" Stephen asked, as if there was a proper etiquette or protocol to adhere to. I asked him if he was okay. The look reminded me of when he was little, when we came home to relieve the babysitter or when the power came back on after a bad storm— part smile, part relief, and part fatigue. I see the shadow of hair on his chin and cheek combined showing the brink of adulthood in contrast with the tear-filled, clumpy eyelashes and freckles from his childhood. I see him at age 3 riding his bike for the first time and then again at 10 when he ice climbed with another friend and his father and was terrified. This is a look I will always remember. "Yes, Mom, the worst part is over. Telling you." I felt so much in those moments, especially the shame in realizing that his worst fear had been rejection from us, the people who had loved him his whole life and all those years before he was born. The worst was over, and we were the worst. I felt like such a terrible mother.

Yet he was smiling, so happy that he would not have to bear his secret alone anymore; he could focus on life again and step out of his bedroom.

"Do you have a boyfriend?" Andrew's question shocked both Ms. Hollos and me, but not Stephen, oddly enough. *Wow*, I thought, *he's putting it all out there on the table for a man who couldn't even utter the word* gay.

"No, Dad, not yet," replied Stephen as matter-of-factly as if he'd been asked if he had homework that night. "I've always just felt different, ever since I can remember. In ninth grade I just sensed I would never be attracted to girls at my school—or girls anywhere, for that matter. I tried for a little while and asked a few girls on dates and dances; well, you know. But, in the end, I just wanted to be their friend, even if everyone else thought they were the most beautiful, smartest, or funniest girl in the class. My response would be a sheepish, 'Well, I'm sorry; I'm just not feeling the vibe," or love or attraction or whatever the word of the month happened to be. You and Dad have always taught me to treat women respectfully, and I always have, which is why I didn't want it to feel like I was leading someone on when I would never want to be more than friends."

I had wanted to ask if he was attracted to anyone and afraid to pursue it, but I thought better of it. We could get his sister to ask him that question in the comfort of our home, not in the guidance counselor's office. I'm relieved he had people at school reaching out to help him and to find his way, especially since we were no help at home.

What was our problem? We had always prided ourselves on being good parents. When Michelle's blue tarp incident occurred, I shared with her a little from my teenage years, something I probably should have done more while she was growing up. We just took for granted that our kids, always good kids, would always make the right decisions. I told her something like this: "Some people have pivotal moments in youth when we recognize the importance of a decision. Not all decisions are little ones leading to the big doozy where everything afterward changes. Small decisions still have great importance. Although I was never the life of the party or particularly chatty, I had a small group of friends I did everything with. I was good at many things but never spent any time specializing in one thing. My mother worried that I was too much of a recluse, so she sometimes pushed me beyond my comfort zone. For example, a boy called to ask me to go bowling in tenth grade. I didn't want to go, so I said no thank you."

Michelle interrupted, asking the same question my mother had: "What were you afraid of?"

138

I explained, "We had just one phone, located in the kitchen, so privacy was rare. I remember heaving a big sigh and saying something along the lines that I was not ready to date. But Mom said"—I put my hands on my hips, mimicking Michelle's tall, feisty grandmother—'This is not a date; this is bowling with a group of friends. Go and have fun.'"

"So, you were very insecure," Michelle said, matter-of-factly.

"Yes, I was. But I called him back, and he sounded happy that I had changed my mind. Bowling that night was indeed fun. I laughed a lot because he was very funny. Bowling turned into another date at the movies, a double feature at the drive-in with friends, and subsequent dates from there. He was the person I shared my first kiss with, right before he left for soccer camp. It wasn't a fireworks moment, because I was too nervous I would screw it up somehow." At this point, Michelle was dying on the couch, laughing, embarrassed by me, her helplessly uncool mother.

Then I changed my tone. "I wasn't ready to have sex yet, but he was; he grew increasingly frustrated when I would say, 'Stop. I'm not ready.'"

"You weren't raped or anything, Mom, were you? Your first time? God, that's awful. Tell me you weren't raped. This is, like, the worst story you could ever tell me!"

"No," I said, almost chuckling to myself. "Thank God he was a good person, but he was also a seventeen-year-old boy with raging hormones, who knew ultimately he wasn't going to get to where he wanted to be with me."

"So, what happened? You're killing me with this story!"

"I broke up with him. On Valentine's Day. End of story."

"What? You broke up with him? Did you tell him how you felt? How you liked him but didn't want to have sex with him yet? If you really liked him, how could you just let him walk away?"

"I knew it wasn't how my first time was supposed to be, not under that kind of pressure and certainly not to keep someone from breaking up with me. That's just crazy talk." I could see that Michelle was thinking about the story, and I felt as if I had disappointed her. "What if I had sex with him before I was ready? What then? Would I always have been willing to have sex because the person I was with wanted to? What about what I wanted? Would I have been more apt to drink or use drugs because someone else thought it was a good idea? Would it have been a good idea to have sex and then maybe be persuaded to have sex without using a condom or another form of protection? Would I have gotten pregnant?"

"Jesus, Mom, what's with all the questions? You go to the bad place too quick! Why do you think it would have been the end of the earth or your life or anything so dramatic? I never would have figured you, of all people, to be so over-the-top about this."

"Well, Michelle, I don't claim to be perfect, but I knew in my heart it was not the right decision, and I wasn't going to let someone else make a decision like that for me. I'm proud of the choice I made then, because it helped me to make other good choices as I grew up."

Michelle shrugged her shoulders.

After we said good-night, I went to the bedroom, pulled off my slippers, and crawled into bed utterly exhausted from the week.

I wonder whether any decision I've made in the last three months has been the right one. Was I being fair to Andrew all those years ago? What signs that Stephen was in crisis had I missed? Am I not the mother and wife I had meant to be all those years ago?

Now Jess and Allison are fighting desperately to save the life of their daughter. What else can we do to help? I've had friends whose children were snatched from them cruelly, and their lives were never the same. I can't imagine a mother's grief in losing a child. Caroline needs to hang on.

35

Michelle

So the preliminary results showed that I'm a donor match for Caroline, and the latest blood work came back positive. Somehow I knew I would be. We've returned to Portsmouth Hospital to complete the marrow transplant, and I'm not going to lie; it feels awesome to know that my marrow could save Caroline's life. Her infection is gone, and the doctors brought her out of the medically induced coma. They seemed optimistic this morning that she had survived the worst, like Stephen, ironically. She needed a donor match sooner rather than later, because her immune system is very compromised and can't handle many more rounds of chemotherapy to keep the cancer from killing her.

I haven't really done anything all that important with my life. So I've started to make promises to myself in the third person, like "If Caroline pulls through this part and Michelle Walker gets to save her life with a transplant, Michelle promises to think more before she acts." There, that about covers every mistake I could possible make regarding future decisions.

We're staying at Jess and Allison's house in Portsmouth, which is an awesome place. I love old houses, especially ones in little cities like this one. I can't live in Lincoln forever. I'm not sure I'll even last until going away to college in a few months. But the point is, I will get to go to college. I will get to make decisions about my future, like where I want to live and who I want to live with, and I'll make mistakes, for sure, and I'll learn from them. But the point is, I get to live. Caroline should get the same chance.

They are only allowing her parents in her room, but I make some silent promises to Caroline along the lines of being a good sister, being a good listener, being someone she can talk to or ski with or hit tennis balls at. She just needs to get better, because we haven't even been introduced, though we share the same genetics and have very loving, fairly decent, although far from perfect parents. We all live in a cool, touristy spot and could visit each other and share photos of ourselves as four little kids. I promise her that Stephen would be awesome to have as a brother and that our lives haven't always been as dramatic and uncertain as they have been in the last year. This would be stupid to say to her, because her life hasn't always been on the verge of ending.

I tell her that from what I've heard, she really has her act together. Perfect grades. Perfect athleticism. Perfect appearance. Loves to read. The whole package. Although Brian tells me she wasn't exactly a happy person even before she got sick, and she didn't have many friends, which seems strange to me for someone who seems so together on the outside … a little bit like my parents.

I tell her that my own family is in need of some quality time together somewhere far away when all of this is over, and she will be a healthy teenager again, ready to enter tenth grade. I tell her that tenth grade was my favorite grade, that she will love it and love everything there is to learn in tenth grade, and that boys aren't nearly as irritating in tenth grade as they were in ninth, and she will get to read coming-of-age novels like *Catcher in the Rye* and *Lord of Flies*.

I realize my family is looking at me as I daydream my promises away to Caroline. They're smiling. Dad says, "Caroline is awake, so you'll meet her soon." Now on to the next phase of wellness. Operation bone marrow donation is a go!

36

Stephen

It's amazing how a crisis can bring a family together—or, in our case, two families. Although it has been only a few days since Dad opened up to me about Chris, from the look on his face alone, I can see an enormous tension has been alleviated. Of course, he feels terrible. He should. He would be a monster if he didn't.

I think about the education we get in school regarding Bystander Theory, which says we have a responsibility to act as citizens of the world, not simply to stand idly by and watch someone be victimized. He participated in making Chris's life miserable and didn't do anything to help when he had the opportunity to. And, ultimately, his anger is what put him in wheelchair. He not only lost a friend, but also part of his innocence and the mobility almost everyone else takes for granted. Good people can have poor judgment, even when not impaired by drugs or alcohol.

Being in a hospital, though, makes me think about people who are truly disabled, people, who unlike my dad, are alone with their thoughts without people to visit them or to take care of them when they get better—if they get better. My dad was really lucky after his accident. He met this guy who also used a wheelchair and was a professional skier. He and a few of his friends, some cranky fellows with mustaches, took my dad on his first few ski lessons, taught him how to ride a handcycle, and showed him that he could still marry a smart, lovely woman and have babies and a career he could be passionate about.

Dad also had an uncle who was paralyzed years ago in a motorcycle accident. As a kid, Dad slept under Gordon's gun rack at his grandmother's house. Gordon was part of a motorcycle club called the Exiles, and one night, while trying to prove he was invincible, he wrapped his motorcycle around a telephone pole after smoking a joint with his girlfriend. Gordon didn't have access to any kind of cool adaptive sports programs like Dad did and therefore spent a lot of time at home alone, battling one pressure sore after another, always with the feeling he wouldn't live that long. He died of cardiac myopathy (also called broken heart syndrome) in his early sixties. That is true disability. Dad said Gordon was incredibly angry and bitter over losing the use of his legs.

Dad is too, despite the exposure to everything he could still challenge himself with and activities we could do as a family. I need to start skiing again for my dad's sake, if nothing else. If we're outside, participating in life, he'll have less time to shut himself off from the world. Plus, I really think he understands how close we were to becoming a statistic, although I'm honest when I say I never thought about taking my own life. I did consider using drugs, but I knew that would never solve any of my real problems. We're going to take better care of each other, especially now that there are more of us. Dad was worried he wouldn't be able to have any children; now he has four he can watch grow up.

When Caroline woke up, we all got to meet her, which was a surreal experience. Mom and Dad were genuine, as I knew they would be. I instantly connected to her, and she smiled through very chapped lips and pale, pale skin. I've talked about being an old soul before, but I think Caroline might have an even older soul than I do.

It felt perfectly natural for me to hold her hand and thank her for sticking around to meet us. "Did I have a choice?" she said. "We've held hands before—in another life, of course. I'll tell you about it sometime." It didn't even strike me as all that odd; I had a feeling that I had known her before, and not just from talking to her family about her.

I knew she was far more badass than any of us Walkers could have imagined. This girl was tough, and she was the reason we had all come together.

The doctors explained the procedure, and despite Jess and Allison's anxious pacing, Caroline looked very calm. With her hands folded in her lap and ponytail in place, she interrupted only once to ask, "So, if this all goes according to plan, and I get well again, when can I play tennis?" Brian held a pillow over her face, and we all laughed.

"You are ridiculous," Brian said. "There might be a chance I could actually beat you while you're getting your strength back." He turned to me and quietly whispered, "She is the most intense athlete I know, which makes her somewhat unfriendly."

"I can hear what you're saying, Brian," Caroline said, smiling. So I know she's used to his sense of humor and doesn't mind it, even when stuck in a hospital room.

They're about to take Michelle to surgery for the bone marrow retrieval. The doctors explained to us that this could happen in one of two ways: either by using a needle placed in the soft center of the bone marrow, also called a harvest, or through something called peripheral blood stem-cell donation, which takes and separates blood from veins in the arm.

The second one is what they've opted to do with my sister. So a few days ago, they gave her a medication to increase the production of new stem cells. Then Caroline will be given a large dose of chemotherapy to treat the malignancy and make room for the new cells to grow.

I did a little research online to better understand how it all works, and, according to the Johns Hopkins Health Library, ablative therapy is what prevents cell production in the marrow, which needs to be empty before the new "stuff" can take root. After the chemo is administered, the marrow is transplanted like a blood transfusion. The new stem cells find their way to her empty marrow and begin reproducing, growing good, healthy cells. Totally cool.

Her blood count will be checked regularly, but doctors should have a good idea if it is successful by two or three weeks after the transfer. Her moms are worried about the many side effects that can occur, but I'm going to be optimistic that there was a reason we all found a way to each other, and it most certainly is tied up in saving Caroline's life, not just prolonging it by a few weeks.

37

Jessie

Standing there in the hospital room, the seven of us surrounding Caroline's bed, I was reminded of the fear I first felt when we adopted those embryos. *Fear* is the best word, because there was so much left unknown about what kind of people created them, about what kind of people they would grow into, if they grew at all. The doctors always prefaced any procedure with a cautionary "Remember, these embryos are a chance at life. They have the potential to grow into children if the timing is right."

These were the last two. They were meant to be, and they were meant to be ours. They were meant to reach their potential for life. This family, the one joining us in Caroline's room, was meant one day to be connected to ours, not because Andrew and Elizabeth wanted to take over parenting our children, but because it does take a village to raise them, just as it did in our parents' generation.

Before Michelle left with Elizabeth to be prepped for her procedure, I hugged her with every muscle fiber in my being. "Thank you" was all I could let escape my mouth before the tears came.

Allison put her arm around both of us and finished the thought for me. "You have been the answer to our prayers."

"It's no big deal," Michelle replied sheepishly. "A little marrow here is the least I can do. One day, when she makes the Olympics or accepts some big award from someone, she can say, 'I'd like to thank Michelle Walker for saving my life,' and then I'll be invited on talk shows; perhaps I'll become a reality TV star, if college doesn't work out for me."

We all laughed, and my fear moved into gratitude for this young woman who was about to save our daughter's life. I was grateful for the parents who raised her, and I was grateful to have the hope that those moments of laughter together were just the beginning.

Michelle and Elizabeth left the room with one set of doctors, and I was left standing there with Allison, Brian, Stephen, and Andrew, with Caroline still the focal point. There was a slight pause while we took in the moment, and then Brian piped up with "Not to make a pleasant moment awkward, but I've got to know, Andrew, why you wouldn't sign the consent for so long?"

"Brian," I snapped, horrified that he was putting Andrew in such a position in that moment. Leave it to my son to put someone on the spot. I knew he wasn't meaning to be rude or confrontational; or maybe he was. Regardless, he was trying to protect his sister. "Andrew, please know you do not owe us any explanation."

Andrew hung his head a minute, and Stephen spoke first. "It's an awfully sad story, if you want to know. I just heard it myself for the first time the other night, and it explains a lot about how my dad has behaved over the last few years—come to think of it, my whole life. Dad, you should tell them the story. We have time, don't we? You need to tell them about Chris." Suddenly, I was eager to hear what Andrew had to say.

Caroline looked at Andrew, and I wondered if she was contemplating letting him off the hook. Andrew breathed deeply and wiped his hands on his blue jeans. Caroline, still studying Andrew's mannerisms, said, "You don't have to explain, but you might feel better. Everyone has their reasons, and yours are just as justifiable as anyone else's. You are clearly not a bad person, and it's obvious that you love your children and wife a lot. Just give us the CliffsNotes version."

"I'm not really sure where to begin," Andrew said. "Let's just say my accident was caused by a poor decision I made when I was about your age. A good friend needed me, and I was too worried about what other people, mostly guys on my soccer team, would think of me. I lacked the courage that you four kids have shown. The thing is, I haven't even told Elizabeth this story yet, and I owe it to her as my wife to tell her next. Then I promise to share the unsavory details of my own adolescence with all of you. Maybe, instead, Stephen could tell you a funny story about our kids when they were small."

"Fair enough," Caroline conceded. "I'd really like to get to know all of you better, but I don't think I could handle another super-serious moment right now. This whole life-or-death situation is getting tiresome, and I'd just like to be entertained, if you would be so kind." She lifted a thin arm to point at Allison and me. "And Moms, stop looking so serious! This is all going to play out just fine. Michelle is going to give me some marrow, and we can get back to normal!"

At that moment, I understood. For months, she had been worried about dying, but not even about her dying, because I'm sure she could handle the emotional trauma of anything. She had worried about what her dying would do to us. She understood we would be destroyed, and the only way she could prevent that from happening was to survive. Even before she was sick, she worried about living. She worried about not being the best. She worried about more than any fifteen-year-old should ever worry about. She lived with the intensity of an athlete hell-bent on being perfect. Now that she has come so close to not being anything, I hope she has learned to laugh more often at herself and maybe make some friends.

I also needed Stephen to tell a lighthearted story to keep me from bursting into tears, and I couldn't make eye contact with Allison. "That's a great idea, Andrew!" I said. "Stephen, please tell us a story to make us laugh. It'll take all our minds off what is yet to come."

Andrew said, "I'll be back in a few minutes. I'm feeling like I need some air, so if you'll excuse me, I'm going to step outside." We watched as he maneuvered through our circle and wheeled out of Caroline's room."

"Is he okay?" I asked Stephen.

"Yeah, he'll be fine. He just has a hard time opening up to people sometimes, even us. My mom calls him an avoider. But I have a story for you." Stephen went on to share the very funny blue tarp incident, which wouldn't be funny to Michelle, so I won't bring it up; followed by the time when he was two and pooped on his front lawn in front of a minivan full of Hasidic Jews staying in a condo next door, followed by his superhero phase of childhood, which lasted a full seven years; followed by the time Michelle announced to her teacher in elementary school that her mom and dad made her in a test tube and that was almost like being as cool as being born on another planet. And so we listened.

38

Allison

Since Stephen was occupying Caroline and Jess, I decided to check on Andrew. I told them I was getting a cup of coffee and would be back shortly. I took the off chance that he might be sitting in the courtyard by the front entrance. Spring had sprung after the longest winter of my life. The cold wind whipped, but the snow had melted. Young daffodils and purple crocuses had popped through the newly thawed earth. Soon, throngs of people would arrive in Portsmouth to sample the summer zest of outdoor dining on decks, ice cream on benches downtown, and lobster rolls near the beach.

I found Andrew sitting in a patch of sunlight caught between two clouds. With his sunglasses on, he looked like he could have been taking a nap.

"Mind if I join you?" I asked.

"No, certainly not," he said. "I mean, yes, you can join me, and, no, I don't mind. Fortunately for me, I always travel with my own seat."

I laughed and pulled up a metal patio chair, which had probably just been brought out of the winter storage that very week.

"Everything okay inside?" he inquired.

"Oh, yes, your son is regaling Brian, Caroline, and Jess with humorous stories from his childhood, and he's a very good storyteller.

Our children seem to have a lot in common. They grow up so quickly, don't they? I feel like it was only yesterday when the twins went off to kindergarten, and now here they are, about to be sophomores, and you have one headed off to college. Does that make you nervous?"

"Nervous, no. Relieved mostly that they have gotten this far in one piece. I was just Michelle's age when I had my accident, which in many ways feels like it was only a few months ago."

"Did your parents think you were going to die? I'm sorry, that is such a personal question, and please don't answer it if you would prefer not to."

"Yes, it was a tough few weeks for them; they weren't sure I would come out of the coma without serious brain damage. No one was wearing seat belts, and the impact of the crash sent me flying from the car into the tree. My spinal cord was severed at T6-T7, and it could have been worse. I could have died, of course, and my friends also could have been killed. Yet they all survived and went on to live lives in other places."

"May I ask you another personal question?"

"Sure, we are raising genetic siblings, aren't we?

"What has been the hardest part about parenting with a disability?"

"The years the kids were babies and then toddlers were the worst, because they didn't understand why my legs didn't work like other people's. Of course, they probably learned to be independent sooner than other kids. I made sure they always took stairs, because someone once told me that people in wheelchairs often have kids who grow up dependent on elevators and ramps, and I didn't want my kids being lazy.

"And I do have some awful memories of being home with them while Elizabeth was teaching night classes and being so worried

154

that I couldn't keep them safe. Like the time Michelle slammed the upstairs bathroom door on her brother's finger. By the time I got myself to the lift and up the lift to get to him, the blood was everywhere. Then there were the grim logistics of getting toddlers to the emergency room. Just getting them from the car into the hospital was stressful. Fortunately, we had good friends in the area I could call to come help me.

"And there was the time Michelle wanted me to help coach her rec soccer team. She must have been eight or nine, and she had heard stories about how much I loved playing as a kid. However, there are certain sports that just aren't as good sitting down as they were standing up. After my accident, I learned to ski and ride a bike and even water ski, but in the sports my kids loved, like soccer and tee ball, I felt like an awful parent."

I nodded, feeling more in sync with Andrew than I could have imagined. "I can say I've always taken mobility for granted, especially when it came to chasing the kids around when they were little. But I do understand the shitty parent thing. We raised both Brian and Caroline to be independent thinkers, not followers, but Caroline has had one issue after another with other girls in her class. She won't even talk about it anymore with us because she doesn't want us going into the school and making waves. We have friends who are teachers there, and they look out for her and keep us posted if things seem to be in a downward spiral, but she's spent so little time there this winter, I'm afraid for her to go back when she's better. It might just be easier to continue tutoring her at home, so she doesn't have to deal with mean girls."

"No, she needs to go back to school when she's better," he interjected. "It's the only way she will learn to develop the tools she needs to deal with people like that, as there will always be people like that in her life, unfortunately. What's the big issue? Why do you think they are mean to her?"

I took a sip from the water bottle that travels with me everywhere and thought about how I wanted to handle that question. "Brian always has had friends and been involved in countless activities and is truly a trendsetter in every sense, but Caroline has allowed other people to make her feel awkward because she has mothers who are lesbians."

"Well, that surprises me with this being Portsmouth and us living in such enlightened times. We have a large population of gay parents in our town as well, but the kids have never said much about it being an issue for their peers; it's a nonissue, except clearly for me."

"I think it's her introverted personality; yet she is so good at so many different things that those kinds of kids who need to capitalize on someone else's weakness have found her Achilles heel. You know how kids can act in a group. I'm sure most of them are perfectly good kids when they're home with their parents and siblings, but put them together in a group, and nastiness ensues. I'm so thankful we didn't have to grow up in this time of social media and textual harassment. I suppose we dealt with other issues, but I always looked forward to going to school.

"Most days, the only part Caroline looks forward to is after-school practice. She is a good student too, an avid reader, great in math, interested in science and history, but she hates to write, because she's so worried about what others are going to think about it. God forbid a peer she isn't comfortable with gets to read it. We always intervened in fifth grade when it started, and even Brian has tried to help her at school with friends and situations that make her uncomfortable. He's just so easy around other people and in all kinds of situations."

"Both you and Jess seem like that kind of person too," Andrew said. "Caroline will find her way through this part of adolescence. Just the fact that you're paying close attention lets her know that you're there in case she needs you. My problem is that I got so caught up in work that I stopped paying attention."

"Andrew, none of us is perfect, and if Caroline pulls through this next procedure, I'm going to see to it that she has more of a life than just that of an intense athlete." I paused. "Elizabeth seems quieter than you. Has that always been the case?"

"For a minute, I forgot that your children come from our genes, and so, yes, it would make sense that Caroline has inherited the less boisterous personality from Elizabeth. However, the up side to that is her observation and intuition skills, which are spot on. I'm not sure what would have happened to our family had it not been for Elizabeth. She pushed and pushed and pushed Stephen to open up to someone, and in the end, it was someone at school. You know, Elizabeth knew years ago that our embryos had been adopted, but she never told me. She was worried about how I would react, and she was right."

"You know, we never worry about Brian the way we worry about Caroline. He just seems to have it all together. Do you have that experience with Michelle and Stephen?"

Andrew chuckled, somewhat embarrassed. "If you had asked me that question a year ago, I would have replied, probably arrogantly, that our children were raising themselves. They didn't really need parents. But in August the shit hit the fan with our two. We had stopped paying attention. Brian may appear to have it all together, and maybe he does for the time being. I was like Brian growing up, involved in sports and having many friends, but I fought insecurity that only certain people knew about. I don't know much these days, but I do know your children need you as ours need us."

The wind picked up, and the sun slipped into the late-afternoon shadow. May is a tricky month in New Hampshire. Wishing I had a warmer jacket, I suggested that we return inside to our families, and so we did. Andrew wanted to check on Elizabeth and Michelle in the recovery room. He predicted she was already asking questions about getting out of the hospital. Those moments with him had taught me more about their family than I ever could have imagined.

39

Brian

Over the next few days, the Walkers returned north so Stephen and Michelle could get back to school. We were in communication daily to let them know Caroline's progress. It's been only eight days, but all signs are good that it will be a success. She gets to come home at the end of next week if everything goes well.

I've decided to paint her bedroom for her as a surprise. It needs some updating, and I've chosen a bright green for a new start. No one, even the graphic artist in the family, wanted to approve my color selection, so it will be a surprise for everyone.

Stephen said he would come down to help this weekend if I trust his painting ability. I told him he would have to prove himself, and I'd let him know. Caroline hasn't liked to do anything with our family, but maybe now that will improve, especially since she can't jump right back into her practice schedule.

Stephen seems like he is going to play the big-brother role, because, well, technically he is my brother, but he doesn't really know me at all. I'm going to invite him down to see the spring musical, *Peter Pan*. I'm Peter, naturally. They weren't sure they wanted to give the lead to a freshman, but I blew their minds at auditions. I'm not as convincing as Captain Hook. I saw a production of this as a little kid; Peter Pan was played by one of my babysitters, Sarah, and she could fly. At least I went around telling people that for months following the performance. She was hooked up to cables, and a team of people helped her to fly. But that didn't matter. I was four, and Sarah could fly.

The story of Peter Pan is a good one too, about growing up. Childhood is magical, blah, blah, blah, but there comes a time when all of us "fly the coop." Not Peter. He doesn't want to grow up or stop playing. That's why acting is so fun; it's playing for big kids.

MJ, aka Momma Jess, wanted to be involved in her school play in middle school and tried out for a small role in *The Wizard of Oz*, but guess what? She wasn't even good enough for a small role. Instead, she was given the role of prompter and lead prop person. If I know my mom, she was the best damn prompter and prop person in any middle school production of *The Wizard of Oz*.

I love singing on stage. I love making people laugh. Mostly, I love telling a good story, and I think that's why history is my favorite subject, other than drama. It's the story of our past; some of it is good and much of it is bad, but the telling of the story makes all the difference. That coupled with the fact that we aren't supposed to make the same mistakes twice. But if entire armies and governments can't do that, how are individual teenagers supposed to?

Take Andrew, for example. Stephen told me the story about his friend who committed suicide. That's not completely Andrew's fault, but he also didn't do anything to help. But he's been paying for that his whole life, and look what it could have done to his family; his accident was just an accident.

Very few people think about little decisions leading to big decisions, leading to even bigger consequences. I have this English teacher, and she talks too much. We do read some great books, but periodically she stops reading and says, "Pencils down. Raise your right hand. I promise that I will not drink and drive a car." Or "I promise I will never break up with a girl or a boy by text messaging." Or, even better, "I promise if someone does not treat me respectfully, I will walk away." Or sometimes she says, "Life Lesson 671: it's important to move away from where you grow up, even if just for a little while."

I know she means well, but I'm only fifteen years old, and I have a good sense of where I'm headed, and especially where I've been. Teachers are strange sometimes. Some I like and respect, and some I just can't stand, but I still have to respect them by the nature their job.

MA (meaning Mom Allison) still meets her first-grade teacher for lunch sometimes. One would think that she would be ancient by now, but she isn't. Mom totally had "transition problems," so Ms. Seidel had to keep an eye on her. Fifth grade to sixth was awful, as was eighth grade to ninth, and then again when she went to college. Ms. Seidel attended Mom's college graduation and came to Moms' wedding, and it was not the first civil union she'd been invited to.

It's strange to think about my parents before they became parents and how they had lives that had nothing to do with my sister and me. MA loves to tell the story of how she streaked through campus her senior year with all of her friends. Thankfully, this was before the Internet. Nobody wants to see evidence of his mother streaking across any college campus, or streaking anywhere, really. She and her best friend took a dance class to fulfill their art requirement senior year, and they are still pissed thirty years later about only getting a B+ on their final paper. They claim it's because they weren't dance majors. I'm not sure either one was a very good dancer, but it was interpretative dance, so it must have been a sight.

MJ was an all-American lacrosse player in college and pretty badass in her own right. Maybe this is where Caroline's competitive edge came from. Mom claims Caroline's work ethic was so strong and she wanted to learn to play the piano so badly in elementary school, she risked life and limb riding her bike past a gigantic Doberman Pinscher to get to lessons. She had to fill her pockets with dog biscuits and chuck them out as the dog approached. Even when the dog dragged her off her bike, she still showed up at lessons with pants torn and shirt muddied. This would be her version of having to walk to school three miles in a driving snowstorm.

My moms did screw up from time to time, but they both turned out just fine, other than being slightly neurotic at times.

I have questions about my biological past, but it looks like I'll have time, and so will Caroline. It's cool to know that I look like someone else, even if she happens to be a woman. Elizabeth is a smart woman, and that counts for something. I think that she and Caroline will understand each other once we all spend a little more time together. Life wouldn't be interesting at all if we always knew what was right around the corner.

40

Caroline

Forty is a significant number. In the Bible, there was rain for forty days and forty nights. Forty hours is a common workweek in Western cultures. Forty weeks is the gestation period of a human baby. There is an Arabic proverb that states, "To understand a people, you must live among them for forty days." That's a good rule of thumb, really. Forty is also the highest number ever counted to on *Sesame Street* and is the number of spaces in a standard Monopoly game. Adults make crazy lists of what they want to accomplish before they reach forty or of what they want to do on their fortieth birthday.

Forty weeks is the amount of time I've been sick or recovering, and now, on this Monday of the forty-first week, I'm headed to play some tennis with Andrew. He told me he was good back in his day but hates it from a wheelchair. The way I see it, if he's ever going to have a chance in hell of beating me, it will be now. Truly, I've guilted him into it; since he almost wasn't willing to meet us in the first place, he owes us!

The day is shaping up into a good one. Seventy degrees and sunny, a little cool for June; a cold front pushed through last night. It's perfect, especially if one is planning on sweating, which I can't wait to do. Moms made me promise I'll take it easy, but I had a good report on my last checkup. Everything looks great; white and red blood cell production is fantastic, not too much and not too little. I'm a regular Goldilocks.

Brian and Stephen are going to paint my bedroom again, as the first color Brian selected made me feel like I was living inside a fish tank that hadn't been cleaned nearly often enough. This new color is better, brighter, and the boys work well together. Elizabeth and Moms are going out for lunch and to some craft fair. I hate craft fairs. However, I'm trying to appreciate what other people enjoy without quite so much judgment. It's going to be a long time before I get my muscles back, but they will grow, and they will be strong again. I will be back next year, better than ever.

Returning to school a few weeks ago was interesting. I thought Moms were going to sit with me in class; their separation anxiety has been ridiculous. However, the day came, and they dropped us off out front and thankfully didn't even get out of the car. Just a wave and a reminder question: "Do you have money for lunch?"

Brian handled that with, "How old do you think we are?" followed by, "Just think, next year, when you buy us our own car, you won't have to drive us to school anymore!" I couldn't help but smile.

People were friendly, for sure, and I didn't spend my usual amount of time trying to figure out if they were being sincere or fake. I was just happy to be there, to be present and accounted for and alive. I had known I'd return there one day and be fine.

I'm not sure if Brian paid a different group of kids to sit with us at lunch, but I didn't care. They were friendly kids, and I recognized a few of the older students from Brian's *Peter Pan* debut. I stayed away from the girls who had never been very kind to me in all the years we had been to school together. Clearly, their internal compass had them stuck at ground zero, because they weren't making much progress in their forward direction of travel.

My speech elective was the last class of the day, a class I had despised, as speaking in front of others was not a skill I wanted to improve. However, I had a story I wanted to tell. Most people had heard about the crazy embryo adoption and subsequent blood marrow transfer, which saved my life, and yes, that is a good story. But this is a better one. "Excuse me, Mr. Thompson," I said to the speech teacher, "you should have us write a persuasive letter on embryo donation. Why is the donation of one's embryos an ethical contribution to society?"

He seemed a little thrown by the assertive version of me, but I think he wanted to encourage the risk I had taken. "Sure, Caroline, that seems like an interesting topic to research further. Could you tell us a little about your experience? That might help people decide how to focus their research. We could even hold a debate on the ethics of embryo adoption."

My classmates murmured actual interest, and so I began. "When people can't have a baby the old-fashioned way, they can get help through fertility treatments. There are a whole bunch of different ways this can happen, but what my moms did was adopt someone else's embryos, someone else's potential for life that they didn't need anymore because they already had two children, which was plenty for them. Honestly, why anyone would want more of us to raise is beyond me." They laughed at my comment because it was, in fact, actually comical.

"Define embryo," Colbie demanded.

"Don't be so dumb," said Ryan. "It's obviously a fertilized egg."

Eunice asked, "When you say *egg*, you are talking about one that has been fertilized by a sperm and would grow into a baby, right?"

Pearce jumped in. "Only if the conditions were right."

"What conditions?" asked Bailey.

"Come on, people," whined an exasperated Kayla. "You all took health in sixth and eighth grade, and you had better know this before we have to take it again as sophomores."

"You know," Chelsey said. "The pH of the mother's uterus, whether the egg implants in the uterine lining, whether that embryo has problems or genetic mutations. Sometimes they just don't implant because they aren't working right. Sometimes they implant, but something still isn't right, and so the mother miscarries, or maybe there is a history of miscarriage, or maybe the mother has an oddly shaped uterus."

"Chelsey, why do you know so much about this?" asked Colbie.

"It's very interesting, and when my mom and I were talking about Caroline's situation, she made the comment, 'It's good they've been so honest with their kids about where they came from, just in case they fall in love with someone who looks just like them.'"

Ben interjected, "Do you mean, like, what would happen if you didn't know what's his name, your biological brother, was your brother, and you fell in love with him?"

"Good thing he's gay, so there's no chance that would happen!" I smiled, and again they laughed.

Maria said out loud what we'd all been thinking. "Wow, this is all a little crazy, huh."

"This potentially could be the best book if you decided to write it one day," Chloe said. "Think about the ethical questions. Think about what if that family hadn't come forward. You could have died, Caroline."

"That's true," I said with the confidence I generally exhibited only when racing or smashing tennis balls. "But I didn't die. I am here, and so are you. The potential energy in this room is unreal, if only we give ourselves a chance to thrive. Then our potential becomes kinetic because we are in motion. The conditions for survival may not always be ideal, and we may take wrong turns and make poor decisions, but the end goal is to continue in the forward direction of travel. To stay the course. To be like Nick Caraway at the end of *The Great Gatsby*: 'And so we beat on, boats against the current, borne back ceaselessly into the past.'"

"Hey, aren't we supposed to read that in American Lit as juniors? Why did you read it early, Caroline?" demanded Eunice. "That makes the rest of us look lazy!"

"Just remember, I had too much time on my hands the last few months, and books were the best company I could have asked for. They didn't bother me with questions or make me eat something I didn't feel like eating. I didn't have to lie to them about how I was feeling to make them feel better. They allowed me to escape into someone else's world for a little while. And I think you're right, Chloe. I think this has the potential to be a great story. Maybe it's my marrow. Maybe it's the way I would make my life, so that I wouldn't 'when I came to die, discover I had not lived.' Maybe my marrow could actually be my marrow."

Mr. Thompson smiled at me, and it's a smile I'll never forget. I think he knew that one day I would write a story others would read. It would be beyond our speeches on integrity or what it means to be an individual or what metaphors best describe adolescence. We all have so much to learn.

I was excited about telling people I believe in reincarnation, as people had visited me in my coma. I now know they were Michelle, Stephen, and Brian in other lifetimes. I sensed their spirits were familiar, and when I woke up, I knew we had been together in a previous life or I had met them in heaven on a previous visit.

For the first time in my life, I'm going to be comfortable with just knowing that and not being able to explain it. Some of us have a better sense of direction than others, maybe because we've lived more lives in other people's bodies. We're all headed in a forward direction. Sure, we may lose our way, but the hope is that by paying attention to each other, we help to reroute the course, so that we ultimately reach our individual true north. The compass's magnetic force will get us only so close; the rest is up to us.

Epilogue

One Man with a Very Old Soul

I died in my sleep peacefully at ninety-six years old. I lived, loved, and laughed until my very last day. My last meal was a strawberry rhubarb pie, because I was so old it didn't matter what I filled my stomach with. My great-grandchildren knew me when I had all of my faculties. Their parents and grandparents brought them to visit me often, even when I had to give up my home and move to the residential facility. I spent my life writing music, performing for people, and traveling the world. If I could come back, I would like to be born in Africa or China. This is my one request.

One Woman with a Very Old Soul

I died in a car accident at seventy-seven. A young woman was texting on her phone while driving and didn't stop in time when the light turned red. But I lived a good life and even saved my sister's life when I was young, just a teenager about to head off to college. I married a man I met while coaching soccer together. We had four children and nine grandchildren. Two of our four children are still married, and two are divorced. I became a high school math teacher who believed math is beautiful. I have no requests for what comes next, because we learn from it all.

Another Man with a Very Old Soul

I died in Iraq when I was only twenty-seven years old. My wife was due to have a baby in four months, and I was supposed to be home by then. I wanted to do something important for my country, and I did. I gave my life, however short it was. I lived strong though. I made the most of each day, loved my family, and never wasted time. My only regret is not living long enough to be a father to my little boy. I knew he was a boy, because I had seen the ultrasound. If I get to come back, I'd like to experience being a father.

Another Woman with a Very Old Soul

I died at fifty-eight in a plane crash, coming back from a book tour for my ninth novel. My husband was with me, as he always accompanied me on trips. We had just celebrated our thirtieth wedding anniversary in New Orleans. We first met at a fundraising gala for adaptive sports. A Paralympic skier, he was the keynote speaker, and I was covering the event for *Sports Illustrated* as a journalist. We fell in love immediately, and I traveled with him, writing as he trained and competed. Due to my many cancer treatments as a kid, we were unable to have our own children and decided after many unsuccessful fertility treatments to be the best aunt and uncle we could be to our many nieces and nephews. If I could come back again, I'd like to be a mom.

ABOUT THE AUTHOR

Heather Krill is a teacher-writer living in the White Mountains of New Hampshire with her husband and children. Having taught middle and high school English for eighteen years, she applied and was awarded a Rotary grant to write a young-adult novel, modeling for her students what it takes to be a writer at work. The idea for *True North* came when she and her husband, Geoff, chose to release their remaining embryos to another family instead of discarding them.

Heather graduated from Connecticut College with a bachelor's in English and earned a master's from Plymouth State University as a K-12 reading specialist. However, her best moments in the classroom come from working with teenagers on finding their own voices through writing. An avid hiker, skier, and reader, Heather brainstorms best when moving her body and mind together in the mountains, rivers, and lakes near her home in North Woodstock, New Hampshire.

Made in the USA
Middletown, DE
07 December 2015